POISONED LOVE

SANAA **DAL**

BALBOA.PRESS
A DIVISION OF HAY HOUSE

Copyright © 2020 Sanaa Dal.

All rights reserved. No part of this book may be used or reproduced by any means, graphic, electronic, or mechanical, including photocopying, recording, taping or by any information storage retrieval system without the written permission of the author except in the case of brief quotations embodied in critical articles and reviews.

Balboa Press books may be ordered through booksellers or by contacting:

Balboa Press
A Division of Hay House
1663 Liberty Drive
Bloomington, IN 47403
www.balboapress.co.uk
UK TFN: 0800 0148647 (Toll Free inside the UK)
UK Local: 02036 956325 (+44 20 3695 6325 from outside the UK)

Because of the dynamic nature of the Internet, any web addresses or links contained in this book may have changed since publication and may no longer be valid. The views expressed in this work are solely those of the author and do not necessarily reflect the views of the publisher, and the publisher hereby disclaims any responsibility for them.

The author of this book does not dispense medical advice or prescribe the use of any technique as a form of treatment for physical, emotional, or medical problems without the advice of a physician, either directly or indirectly. The intent of the author is only to offer information of a general nature to help you in your quest for emotional and spiritual well-being. In the event you use any of the information in this book for yourself, which is your constitutional right, the author and the publisher assume no responsibility for your actions.

Any people depicted in stock imagery provided by Getty Images are models, and such images are being used for illustrative purposes only. Certain stock imagery © Getty Images.

Print information available on the last page.

ISBN: 978-1-9822-8180-9 (sc)
ISBN: 978-1-9822-8182-3 (hc)
ISBN: 978-1-9822-8181-6 (e)

Balboa Press rev. date: 07/16/2020

For Faizy,

Without that silly bet we made a few years ago,

I'd never have written this story.

It is because of your motivation (and the countless times I promised this book for your birthday), that my readers are reading this.

It is because of you, that I decided to take a risk and publish,

I hope it was worth the wait x

Can't express my gratitude for your help, your advice during my numbness.

Times when I though you would have to finish the story for me,

In hopes I'll be there to hand you this myself,

And if not, I leave you my words:

Stop being so harsh on yourself. Stop trying to make other people proud. Instead think about how much you've done, how much you've helped people. How much you helped me.

Because I can guarantee one thing. If you didn't answer my calls in the middle of the night all those times that I was contemplating....

My old habits would have been the death of me. Thank you for being an amazing friend x

Chapter 1
Confidence?

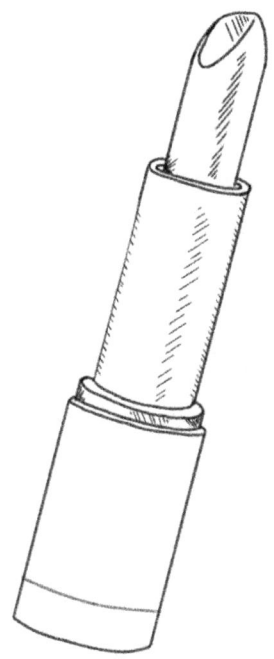

It's okay to be confident....
Just don't lose yourself for others.

I felt a bit odd at first.

It was the first day back to school and I was in my second year of college/sixth form. Just that morning, I decided to forget about everything: forget about what people thought of me, what they expected of me. And honestly, I did not care whether they judged me. That was supposed to be my year and I wasn't going to be the same, quiet Amy again. I wanted to be different - a person who'd stand out and be remembered. And clothes made a huge impression.

Before this, I would have regarded myself as "normal". But by changing the way I dressed, by faking my confidence, by pretending I was the most secure and happy person, I knew I was creating a mirror. One which contradicted everything I used to be.

I guess the word *normal* was a bit of an overstatement after what happened at the end of last year. Thankfully, that wasn't common knowledge.

I woke up, way earlier than I'm used to.

My clothes were hanging on my cupboard handle. I jumped out of bed and quickly went to the bathroom. I came out and rushed to my dressing table, running all around my room grabbing everything I needed to look perfect. I wasn't trying to appear indecent. Yes, I wanted all the guys' attention on me, but my intent wasn't to

It's okay to be confident....
Just don't lose yourself for others.

sleep with all of them. I just wanted to be confident. I was tired of being overlooked and considered vulnerable because of the clothes I wore and, the fact that I hadn't done as much sexual stuff as others had. I just wanted to prove everyone wrong. Doesn't everybody?

My face was artistically drawn with make-up. I had never been so focused on getting ready. But this time, my make-up was dark. I decided to rebel against my usual light look, which was a bit of blusher and lip gloss. That didn't even seem like an option anymore. I opened my Urban Decay palette that I had gotten as a present and never thought I'd use and applied the darkest eyeshadows in the palette. I stuck on the fake eyelashes and put on my cherry-red lipstick. My highlighter was popping, my foundation was flawless and my contour was perfection. I thought all of this was going to make me feel happy, make me feel satisfied, but to be honest, I felt like I was dying trying to be someone I wasn't.

I put on my pure-white blouse, leaving a button undone and pulled on my tights and short skirt. I got a blade and ripped my tights so they looked like ripped jeans, just a lot more provocative. And I didn't care. Not a single bit. I pulled my hair out of my flat pony-tail. The idea of red hair extensions seemed out of the ordinary for me, it was perfect. I clipped them in before curling my vividly coloured hair.

It's okay to be confident....
Just don't lose yourself for others.

I was ready. My clothes, my makeup, my hair- the only thing left was shoes. Yes, I could've worn black flats. But why would I go so far to look a certain way only to wear plain shoes? I rummaged through my shoe drawers until I found the perfect pair: black glossy stiletto heels. I'd say at least a good four or five inches. There were dark red laces that crossed the shoes. And instantly, I fell in love. I'd never worn those shoes before. The shoes still had the receipt. It was a match made in hell.

I walked down the stairs with my dark red side bag. I looked somewhat like a bright goth: a white blouse. But dark makeup.

Just as I reached the door, my mum approached me.

"Amelia?"

"Yeah. Mum?" I replied, slowly turning around. I honestly had no idea what her reaction would be like. Would she shout? Would she tell me to go get changed again? Would she even care? My parents weren't very predictable.

"Oh my God!" she gasped; her hand dramatically placed over her chest.

My heart started to beat faster. I couldn't say I was very close to my parents; they were always going out, so I'd just constantly be getting on with my own things. They were estate agents for high-end properties across

It's okay to be confident....
Just don't lose yourself for others.

the world, so they travelled a lot. And I was also an only child, so growing up playing with a babysitter was *much fun.*

"Jack! Get over here now!"

My dad came running from the kitchen with a spatula and a pan with egg in it. He must have thought there was an intruder. I didn't know if I was more scared about what my parents would say or if I'd just burst out into laughter because of the way my dad came stumbling.

The sound of a huge clank numbed all our ear-drums as his pan fell and his egg splattered all over the floor.

"What on earth?" he yelled.

My mum came over and hugged me. My dad smiled awkwardly.

"My little princess Amelia?" Dad asked in a happy tone that was weirdly laced with a sort of sadness.

"Finally," Mum sighed happily. She stopped hugging me after a bit; I was glad when she moved away. We'd never hugged, so when we did it was very uncomfortable.

"What?" I replied confused.

"We've been waiting for this honey; you finally came out of your shell."

"We?" Dad questioned.

It's okay to be confident....
Just don't lose yourself for others.

Mum rolled her eyes, "Yes, we've," she turned to my dad. "You keep saying how she's too shy. So, if this is how Amelia becomes confident, then let it be. She wasn't always going to be your '*sweet little princess*' forever." Mum used an almost mocking tone.

Dad was flustered and shouted over her voice, "Never talk bad about my sweet little princess title!"

My father was like a little child. My parents were complete opposites. And I always found it hilarious. But it wasn't their different personalities that stopped me from being close to them.

Trying to get through each day was tough last year because of what was happening at school, especially as I didn't know how to confide in my parents about it. That's where I ended up exerting most of my energy. And it created distance between us.

They found it hard to understand how important friendships were to me and what kind of mental effect it'd had on me. Now don't get me wrong; I loved my parents. They weren't strict, and they didn't just leave me isolated. They did try to connect with me, mostly because I was in my teenage years. And we did. We did talk. We did connect. And I liked it when that happened. But recently, with all the stress from my schoolwork and friends and my social anxiety, I'd been withdrawing into myself.

It's okay to be confident....
Just don't lose yourself for others.

"You do you know you're going to get done, right?" my mum said, half laughing.

Dad replied so defensively, "You think? This is going against so many of the school's policies."

I knew it just came as a bit of a shock to him.

"But I just think you should do one more button honey," my dad said sheepishly.

"Oh let her be a teenager, will you? Didn't you fall for me when I dressed with a little skin showing?" she winked at him, Dad smiled at her and didn't bother arguing.

"Nope, too cringe," I said laughing as I walked out the door.

The whole time I was walking to school, everyone kept staring at me. Constantly. They'd look once, turn away, and with shock, would look again with their eyes threatening to come out of their sockets. A lot of people were surprised, and I was okay with that. To be honest, it made sense to be confused when you saw a person like me wearing such clothes and carrying such confidence.

The silent yard that I was welcomed with made my steps falter and eventually stop.

"How dare you!" were the first words I heard.

"How dare you come into college like that!" oh shit. I was

It's okay to be confident....
Just don't lose yourself for others.

about to get done. I knew immediately I was going to be in a *lot* of trouble.

I was terrified. Not because I was getting into trouble but because I was trying to be confident. I was trying to be a new person, and getting called out like that had the potential to embarrass me and finish things before they even started.

"Follow me. Now!"

With fear in my eyes and my legs starting to shake, I lowered my head and started walking behind the head teacher. Knowing very well that everyone was staring at me, I didn't even dare look up. Even the regular subject teachers were speechless.

I walked through the hallways and past the classrooms until I reached the far end of the school, where the head teacher's office was. She opened the door and tried to make eye contact, but I just went in after her and sat down. She cleared her throat and claimed her throne before me, which she then adjusted for a good minute. It was like being with Goldilocks: not too high; not too low. As she saw me smiling a little from her spending so much time fiddling with her chair, she realised how awkward it became for her, and without wasting any more time, she started talking.

"Now Amelia," she said in a concerned tone.

It's okay to be confident....
Just don't lose yourself for others.

I finally made eye contact with her.

"Yes. Miss?" I replied cautiously.

"Are you seriously asking me that question. Amelia?"

I stayed silent in embarrassment. What I said was barely even a question.

"You know the school dress code."

"Yes Miss," I replied in shame because I knew she was right: the way I was dressed was way too inappropriate for college.

"You've never been in trouble before; you are a straight-A student who doesn't get distracted. And I know you're friends with one of the popular girls, Piper Jackson? I think. But dressing this way to be 'popular' is unacceptable."

Her voice began fading out, I started to drift off, thinking how my big impression of being confident went so small. I looked around her quirky room from the corners of my eyes whilst also making eye contact with her every once in a while, but she wasn't too concerned about maintaining eye contact either. She kept lowering her gaze to the floor and it really confused me, but I just carried on daydreaming. I looked at the clock, it had been twenty minutes, I had no idea how much shit she could have been talking for twenty minutes. I started

It's okay to be confident....
Just don't lose yourself for others.

focusing my attention on the items she had on her desk and the wall behind her.

I had never been in her room before, and it was not what I expected. I could very easily tell she *loved* fashion. She had several Vogue and other magazines of the month, half her makeup on one side of her desk -about two pencil cases full- and a pair of black velvet heels (On her desk!); And she was telling me I was inappropriate.

"Amelia?"

"Sorry... what?" I asked confusedly, I was regretting drifting off into my own thoughts. I'd made my situation even more uncomfortable.

"What do you say?" she asked curiously.

"I'm sorry could you please repeat the question," I felt bad for annoying her, but then again, she didn't have to give me a huge lecture. She could have just told me my punishment and we both could have just carried on with our day of school.

She sighed -but not in anger- it was a sound of annoyance and desperation

"You are allowed to wear makeup and your clothes instead of a uniform, after all, you are in Sixth Form. But from tomorrow, don't wear a practically shear blouse with ripped tights unless you're gonna wear a

It's okay to be confident....
Just don't lose yourself for others.

longer skirt and a jacket on top. It makes the school look unprofessional."

I was so confused and taken aback by her calm response, I started to concentrate on every word she was saying.

"Just tell me one thing."

"Yeah...?" I asked not wanting to know.

"Where did you get those shoes from?" she asked in an innocent and awe-filled tone.

I had no idea what to think. She acted kindly to me so I assumed it would have been fair of me to tell her where the shoes were from? It made sense, she adored fashion, and then I realised, that was why she kept looking down. To admire my shoes. I wasn't complaining. If I got to wear the dark makeup, and tone down the indecency of my clothes a little, just because she wanted to know where the shoes were from, I was fine with that. I was more than fine with that. It was such a relief.

With a sense of consolation, I replied, "Umm, they're from Meltops, miss."

"Thank you, Amelia," she said with a look of ease in her eyes.

I walked out of her office feeling a jar of emotions: confused, relieved, happy, embarrassed, and anxious. Anxious as hell. I was worried about walking into class

It's okay to be confident....
Just don't lose yourself for others.

late, the attention that had already been drawn by my costume heightened my apprehension of walking into the classroom mid-lesson.

Taking my heels into account, I tiptoed to the door of the classroom trying to organise the chaos in my head. On the first day back to school/college, we usually spent the first half of the day until lunch with our form classes. I came to a stop outside the classroom- petrified to walk in. I knew I wouldn't be getting into trouble for my clothes, the headteacher had probably sent out an email to the teachers about not paying too much attention to my inappropriate clothing for the day.

I started practising all the ways I could enter.

"Sorry I'm late," and just go sit down.

Or

"I'm so sorry I'm late, I was in Mrs Beetles office."

I did this for a few minutes, fidgeting my fingers and shuffling my feet, trying to think of the least embarrassing ways I could walk into the class.

A creaking sound broke my train of thought.

I turned- ever so slowly towards the door, hoping that what I was thinking wasn't true. But it was.

It's okay to be confident....
Just don't lose yourself for others.

This guy from my class came out. And he had had a rather good glow-up during the holiday, I'd never found him so attractive. I halted my racing mind and awkward movements to take him all in.

His name was James Bridge. He had dark black hair; it was long but looked a little short because of how his hair was wavy. His eyes were green. Emerald green. When my eyes found his, I got lost into his gem-like orbs.

"Ahem," he said like he was trying to get my attention. I immediately broke the eye contact and snapped back to reality.

"Mr Price is calling you inside," he informed me, smiling slyly yet dominantly. But just as he went back into the classroom, he glanced at me, from my high heeled shoes to my hair extensions. I felt a knot in my stomach. There was something about the way he looked at me like he wanted me but in a respectable way, not like those boys who go sleeping with every girl simply for sexual pleasure.

I walked in after him.

"If you're done with the role-playing Amy?" Mr Price questioned looking a little stressed, it was probably because of how many sheets and notices and time tables he had to give out. I then realised that meant the whole class heard my practising impressions of trying not to

It's okay to be confident....
Just don't lose yourself for others.

be embarrassing, but it made the whole situation more awkward.

My cheeks became as red as the colour of my lipstick. I lowered my eyes and walked to the back of the classroom where my friends were sat. As I walked to the table, I could hear everyone murmuring and my friends giving me a certain stare - urging me to hurry up.

I sat down at the table. Mr Price started going around the classroom giving out stacks of sheets to the students, whilst people's chatter filled the silence that my entrance brought to the room. I glanced at James's perfect features, but he wasn't looking at me, he was talking to his friends. I was just mesmerised by him.

My attention was snapped back to the group of people sat in front of me as all of my friends started to ask so many questions.

"What made you decide to come to school; like this?" Piper asked confusedly

"Are you feeling okay?"

"What is going on?"

The questions overwhelmed me and with my morning being as eventful as it was, I was in no mood to repeatedly explain myself. My gaze drifted as my mind yearned for a little solace among the chaos and I

It's okay to be confident....
Just don't lose yourself for others.

involuntarily fixed my eyes to one thing; James. When he turned around, I looked away really quickly, but something made me look back at him, he smiled and winked.

I felt uncomfortable but also felt a desire. I couldn't really explain it because I hadn't come to grips with it myself. I liked him, but I didn't like the way his expressions made me feel - as though I had no control.

I looked away again. And I distracted myself by answering some of the many questions my friends were asking.

The bell finally went, Mr Price sighed with annoyance.

Some people went off for their first lesson but my friends and I had a free lesson, so we headed to the break room.

"I'll give you the rest of the sheets and notices tomorrow!"

The world around me just drowned out. I was focused on James' breath-taking green eyes, and the way he talked to me, and the way he looked at me like I was something precious to him and something that he desired.

I just loved the way he looked at me.

And I desired him...

It's okay to be confident....
Just don't lose yourself for others.

Chapter 2

Desires

Without the leap of faith,
You'll never know what could have been.

For lunch, I sat down next to my friends, but my attention was nowhere close to them. I sat across the hall just trying to make eye contact with James, who also had a free lesson and was there, metres away from me.

"Amelia, so what happened? Amelia?" Cece asked with a dying curiosity.

She was the curious one in my friendship group. There were four of us:

Cece was known for her curiosity- out of the four of us in our friendship circle, she would always be the one with the questions. She didn't like it when she couldn't understand things- certainly would be the first to die in a horror movie. Apart from her, there was Piper -who technically used to be my best friend. She and her brother were the most popular in the entire school and sixth form. And Hayley- whose first language was sarcasm.

"He's so, so, just so fit." I nonchalantly murmured, staring into absolute air.

I had no idea I said that out loud. All three of them then turned their gaze to where mine previously had been.

"Wait, what?" "Who?" "Amelia?" All the questions of confusion resurfaced the conversation as soon as I had made that daydreamed thought about James. A thought

*Without the leap of faith,
You'll never know what could have been.*

that should've stayed a thought and never should have come out as words.

"Oh my god, James Bridge?" Cece guessed.

I giggled in an attempt to dodge the question.

"Yes, James Bridge," I said with an exasperated sigh.

Everyone was overjoyed with me crushing on a guy after what seemed like so long, but Piper seemed a little off. She was sat with us, but it felt like she didn't want to be sitting with us. As though she had been forced to. But I knew why.

Ever since I talked to her about how I had been feeling at the end of year 12 (last year), she began to drift away from me. I knew what I'd told her was shocking- I guess she just got tired of me, after all, she'd been spending a lot more time with Charlotte than me. Charlotte wasn't in our friendship group- and sadly by the looks of it, I didn't think Piper would have been in a few months either.

"So... just go ask him out?" Hayley spoke out of nowhere.

"Omg, yah, you totally should. Besides, you look gorgeous today- how could he say no?" Cece argued.

Without the leap of faith,
You'll never know what could have been.

"Ugh, okay, it's not like I have much to lose," I replied, trying to be the new confident person that I wanted to be. Maybe the new Amy was one who didn't overthink things and took risks.

"Yes, go Amy!" Hayley replied ecstatically.

I got out a piece of paper and a pen and began writing on the paper like they do in the movies.

Will you go out on a date with me?

| Yes | No |

I folded the piece of paper whilst all my friends watched in eagerness, as though a new episode for their favourite TV show was about to come out.

I walked towards the table that James was sat at with his friends. As I walked there, a few people from all the other tables were still looking and talking about me to their friends. I finally got to James's table after what had felt like forever.

When I reached the table, he and all his friends swivelled their heads towards me in confusion. I was hugely out of my comfort zone. I gulped.

"Can we help with you something?" a random boy from the table spoke. I'd started getting all nervous

Without the leap of faith,
You'll never know what could have been.

and worried. I could feel my hands getting sweaty. So, before I could make the situation worse, I quickly spoke.

"Um, yeah, I just wanted to give this to James."

I handed the piece of paper to James and hurryingly, walked off before any of the boys could have commented on the awkwardness of the situation. I didn't dare to look back to see if he had opened the paper, or if he was laughing at it. I was so fear-stricken that he and his friends would ridicule me.

I went back to the table where all my friends were and sat down with a nervous sigh.

"So? What did he say? Omg did he say yes?" Cece and Hayley both started questioning at once.

"What? No."

"He said no! How's that possible."

"I mean no he didn't say yes. But he didn't say no. I mean I don't know. I just handed the paper to him." I cleared the confusion desperately.

"And you didn't wait for a reply?" Hayley was disappointed.

"Hey guys, I'm going to go now- Charlotte's calling me," Piper spoke out of the blue. I smiled at her, but I could

Without the leap of faith,
You'll never know what could have been.

see she didn't want to be around us. Everyone said bye as Piper walked off and the commotion started again.

"Omg, Amy, he's coming. Get ready. Put a sexy smile on," Cece whispered.

Hayley disagreed, "No, don't smile. Pretend you're talking to us and start biting your lip. My exes loved that kind of stuff."

Cece and Hayley gushed over my 'preparation' in the short time it took for James's log legs to reach our table. But I didn't know how to do all of that. They could do it because they were experienced, and I wasn't exactly anywhere near that. I was going over a million thoughts in my head, contemplating whether I should smile, bite my lip, sit up, slouch down, seem like I didn't care. There was so much I could do but my brain and my mouth seemed to lose their coordination just when I needed it most.

"Please don't say no…"

What the actual heck! I wanted to slap myself. My reply made me seem like a needy cow who wanted to desperately go out with him. All my friends watched and cringed in pity for me. I got so flustered with what everyone was telling me to do that I came out with the most desperate response a girl could have given. But James just chuckled.

Without the leap of faith,
You'll never know what could have been.

"Don't worry, my answer is yes, Jasmine."

Wait. What? I thought. And Cece thought. And Hayley thought. Who the fuck was Jasmine?

"Excuse me!" I yelled, rowdy enough that a few people turned around. My friends all lowered their gaze, thinking I was about to start an argument, and knowing exactly what could have happened if I did.

"Aha, I'm just kidding love. I know you're Amelia," James continued.

I breathed a sigh of relief as my body relaxed. So, he was the joking kind. It was a funny joke. Just very blooming unexpected.

"I loved your reaction though. You seem like a very feisty girl when you want to be. I think I might just call you Jasmine all the time." He carried on talking with a beautiful smile and occasional chuckles in between.

"Wait for me after school today. You know. For a date," he flashed the piece of paper in front of me.

"Yes. Of course," I very formally replied.

He walked off, putting the piece of paper into his pocket and turned around giving me that *look* once again before biting his lip and walking back to his table.

Without the leap of faith,
You'll never know what could have been.

"Did he just bite his lip?" Hayley asked. Everyone started laughing and was overjoyed.

Cece continued, "And Amelia, what on earth was with the 'Please don't say no'." We were giggling and laughing uncontrollably.

"Can you believe the whole Jasmine thing?" Hayley said in mid laughter. We all carried on talking- catching up about the summer holidays till the bell went for the next lesson.

After lunch I had psychology. And I hadn't spoken to Piper since lunch. The school day had come to an end, but my day with James was about to begin.

We went to the local café not too far from our school. He paid for my coffee and was so polite and funny the entire date.

"So, Jasmine. Jaz. Jazzy. I think Jazzy matches you quite well. You've just got a funny jazzy vibe don't ya?" he laughed and my giggles followed straight after.

I wasn't very sure what to say so I thought I'd come up with a pet name for him.

"Well, James. Jamey. Jam." I uneasily came up with.

"Jam?" he so curiously questioned. We both burst out laughing and it felt as though the tension had gone. You could say the conversation was, well, spread smoothly...

Without the leap of faith,
You'll never know what could have been.

The rest of the date went so well. He was also a single child, always going out with his friends. However, I also noticed he didn't have much of an empathetic side, I mean he didn't seem to be very understanding of people's emotions. I realised that when he got a little frustrated by this drunk woman who we saw crying on the way home. But all of that aside, our date went quite well, and he walked me home.

I decided to tell my parents all about my day and they seemed thrilled that I started to talk to them more. I was so happy. James was so funny and charming. I thought after what happened last year, I'd never be able to move on in life.

Without the leap of faith,
You'll never know what could have been.

Chapter 3
First Real Love

You'll know what true love is;
When you see nothing but perfection in them.

It had already come to the end of the first week of school. My first week of year thirteen. My last year before going off to university. And I felt like a different person. A stronger, more confident, and more fashionable girl.

Everyone was talking about the *new* me, luckily no one but Piper knew about the past me. Well a certain phase of the past me.

It was Saturday and James and I made plans to watch a movie at cinemas. I was so excited; we had spent so much time with each other throughout the week and I was hopeful about how things would turn out. I felt like things were going well. I was just really falling for James.

"Amelia!" my mum yelled from down the stairs. I swiftly ran out of my bedroom quickly glancing at myself once more in the mirror making sure my clothes, hair, and makeup looked perfect. I went down the stairs and saw James waiting for me in my overly modernised living room.

"Yeah, so I'm looking to go pro...' he conversed with my dad.

Dad and James seemed to be getting along very well from what it looked like. I just wished my dad wasn't doing his '*fake kindness to find dirt on you to prove to my daughter you're a prick and not good enough for her*' act.

You'll know what true love is;
When you see nothing but perfection in them.

He had done this with a few guys I went out with a few years ago and the relationships never did end well.

"Amelia," Mum whispered in the corridor outside the living room. I went to her.

"Hurry up and get your lad away from your father before poor James is killed by your dad's crazy interrogation." We both laughed at how correct she was.

I went inside the living room, grabbed James's hand, and said, "Sorry Dad, James, and I will miss the movie if you don't let him leave." I laughed to brighten the atmosphere and before my dad could respond, I dragged James out of the house in the most subtle way I could run away from my dad. I'm sure Mum was laughing as James and I got out briskly.

We got to the cinema pretty quickly. It was a small walk from my house. Our conversation the whole way flowed so easily. We even discussed the food we wanted at cinemas.

"Two tickets to see Fast and furious and one nachos tray please," I spoke over the counter.

"That'd be £17:20 please," the woman over the counter answered. I quickly handed a twenty note and collected the tickets and food.

You'll know what true love is;
When you see nothing but perfection in them.

"Keep the change!" I yelled as I speedily walked off before James could click on. He followed me and then abruptly stopped.

"No! Hang on a minute. Wait. Why did you payyyy? You should have let me!"

I just smiled and walked to the theatre.

"Hey, Jazzy. Nope, won't let you get away with this!" he began poking and tickling me, which was difficult since we were both standing. My giggles followed and the nachos tray was shaking.

Laughing breathlessly, I said what hopefully sounded like, "Stop... I'm so ticklish!"

We were both laughing hysterically, his eyes fixed on mine and everyone's eyes fixed on our childish behaviour. But it didn't matter. His smile was worth all the judgemental stares.

"Be quiet!" someone from the front yelled.

"Amy, do you trust me?" he randomly asked.

"Yes..."

"Follow me."

"But what about the movie?" I asked as he threw the tickets into the bin whilst walking out of the theatre.

You'll know what true love is;
When you see nothing but perfection in them.

"I think we should go somewhere else. Just come with me," he was about to throw the nachos too.

"Oh, hell no! Nachos belong in my stomach, not in the bin," I argued at his attempt to throw it away.

"Haha, only for you Jaz," he handed me the tray. I felt a little embarrassed after saying that since that was something the old shy me would have never said to a guy. But I carried on following him.

We walked out of the cinemas and we took a bus to the countryside, where we stopped and admired the natural beauty until…

"Right, shall we?"

"Shall we what?" I asked.

"Well, I haven't brought you to take a stroll around some trees. You see that grey bricked house?", which he then pointed to.

"No one's step foot in that house for forty years love. We're gonna change that."

I was gobsmacked, "Say what? I'd rather not get a heart attack from a haunted house if that's okay with you?" I nervously laughed.

"Jaz, don't stress. Trust me. I'll make it worthwhile…" there was something hypnotic about the way he said

You'll know what true love is;
When you see nothing but perfection in them.

that line. I felt no reason not to follow him and my footsteps seemed to subconsciously follow his.

We came closer to the house. I was putting on my best smile and trying to pretend that my legs weren't wobbling in fear. But he grabbed my hand and turned his head slightly towards me.

"It's okay, Amy. I'm here right by your side." His words hushed my racing heart as we loosened the eye contact, and he helped me climb over the fence.

We entered through the typical brown creaky door. It was exactly like a horror movie. Stairs were the first thing that met our eyeline. And it was the first place James walked towards. His hand that held mine was powerlessly yet so intimately pulled along with him.

"This place is giving me the chills," I mumbled as we walked up the unstable stairs.

"Would this make it feel better?" he replied

"Would…" I lost my words in my throat as he leaned in. His hand moving from my hand to my waist and one hand on my neck. His eyes drifted to a close as he came closer and his lips softly touched mine. He then moved back, our eyes opening at the same time.

It was our first kiss, and as much as he tried to calm me, him coming so close to me… it was radiant.

You'll know what true love is;
When you see nothing but perfection in them.

"Regretting coming here?" with a daring smile he asked.

"Hmm, I'm not sure, I think the ghosts here could be perving on us." I humorously added.

"Let them…" his lips reattached back on to mine. More locked on than the previous.

We toured the entire house; I was still a little afraid but he held my hand with a stronger grip after the kiss. I felt protected and safe with him.

When it began getting dark, we caught another bus back to town where he walked me off. It felt like the perfect ending to the craziest day.

"Did you have fun. Even though you were scared shitless?"

"You could tell?" I laughed and looked down in regret.

"You ain't an actress. I could feel your pulse, faster than a roller-coaster the entire time I held your hand in the house."

"Aha. I didn't know you were monitoring my pulse. *You a doctor now?* but yes, I had a great time and somehow, I think it was better getting to kiss you in a place where we could have died! But it was a good thrill. Thank you," I replied gratefully for the day's adventure

You'll know what true love is;
When you see nothing but perfection in them.

"No problem Jaz. I like you a lot, I'm surprised I've never talked to you before, but it's fine; I want to do a lot of crazier things and hold your hand through them."

"Should I be worried Jammy boy?" I asked

"Ah, the Jam has re-emerged as my name. And no... simply be excited."

We kissed each other goodnight as we departed for the evening.

You'll know what true love is;
When you see nothing but perfection in them.

Chapter 4
She's different

James Bridge

*Stop trying to be like everyone else.
Being different is rare, like rubies amongst the dust.*

I came back from my date with Amy and went straight to where the guys were hanging.

I felt a sort of calmness within me after spending time with Amy. There was just something about her. She was different. I walked in without knocking. All the guys' houses are like second homes to us. We all know where everything is. We're all comfortable with each other's families. For me, it was like having one big family.

"James, you're here!" one of the lads called out to me.

"Yeah, I just got back."

Everyone was sat around a table drinking beers and eating nachos.

"Why is everyone obsessed with nachos?" I asked bewildered. I didn't get a reply, just laughter.

"Forget the nachos, tell us how it went with that chick, Amelia. You guys went out on a proper date again, right?" Malcolm, who was sat in the centre of what seemed like a circle of the guys, questioned.

I spoke about Amy like she was the first girl I'd ever been out with.

"Man, she's so funny, a little bit shy and modest which is just perfect because she isn't like those girls who dress and behave for attention. She's pure."

Stop trying to be like everyone else.
Being different is rare, like rubies amongst the dust.

"The fuck do you mean by that James?" one of my mates yelled out. Everyone started laughing wildly.

"I think she is you know. I think she's still a virgin." I carried on.

"You, one of the most popular guys in school, wants to be seen with an innocent little virgin?" Malcolm asked.

"She isn't that kind of virgin, and maybe she isn't fully comfortable around me. But she's opening up. And she makes me feel wanted. Not like those girls who use you to show off to their mates. She makes me want to impress her. I can't explain how beautiful and free-spirited she is."

"Do you actually like her or are you tryna sleep with her James. Cuz, the way she looked the other day, God damn I wouldn't blame ya," someone else questioned, whilst everyone nodded and laughed in agreement.

"No, well...yes, she's absolutely stunning but I don't want to rush her, we're already sort of a thing, so I'm not worried about her leading me on." I saw that Malcolm looked down after I said, probably because he remembered Ella when I said it.

"Her opinions matter to me, I can't explain it. Every time we've hung out it has never been even remotely similar to my exes. I know it started as lust with the clothes she was wearing, but nah, I see something more with her."

Stop trying to be like everyone else.
Being different is rare, like rubies amongst the dust.

"Alright then, just don't do what I did," Malcolm made a very dark humoured joke, there were a few stifles of chuckles. It was funny but the lads weren't sure if they should have been laughing at such an incident.

For the rest of the night, before I went back home, my mates and I just carried on talking and drinking a bit. I was ecstatic to see Amy again the next day. We'd made plans to meet again for another date, but this time it was going to be a little late during the evening.

Stop trying to be like everyone else.
Being different is rare, like rubies amongst the dust.

Chapter 5

A drop into the past, A step forward?

James Bridge

*Learn to embrace your past,
Not forget it.*

It was Sunday evening and Amy and I had plans to meet again but it was going to be more of a late-night date. Nothing was going to happen of course; It was a school night! Just kidding, she meant a lot more to me than just sex, I didn't care if I had to wait months to sleep with her, as long as I could genuinely spend time with her with no bullshit.

I arrived at her house and she was already standing outside waiting for me.

"Not even gonna get an invite in?" I joked around.

"Trust me Jammy boy, if I invited you in my dad would bore you to death with another interrogation, I'm saving you from his stupidity at this point," she started laughing.

I looked at her with wonder in my eyes, smiled then said, "Aha don't worry, my parents are *way* worse."

"Someone's worse than my dad?" she replied sarcastically.

We talked a lot on the way to the pier, where we bought popcorn and candyfloss from the closing stalls. Everything was bright with all the lights- (the lights stayed on all night), but the tents and stalls had started to pack up.

Learn to embrace your past,
Not forget it.

"Everything's kind of closing, there's not much we can do, you got any ideas?" I asked.

"Oh, come on James, we don't need to go on typical movie dates to have fun. Just sit next to me on the pier and watch the beautiful sea crash on the lonely beach with me. Let's appreciate nature as it takes place before us and cherish the moment together."

Amy didn't mind those simple dates. She was into those dates where you didn't do much except appreciate the time spent together. And I loved that about her, all my exes expected me to take them somewhere different every single time and wanted me to pay for everything every time. Like I'm 18, I ain't got 1.8 million to my name! I guess that was another thing that made Amy special, she wasn't choosy, little things made her happy and that's what made her so precious.

"So, you're the tranquil kind?" I added.

"Tranquil?" Amy asked in an intrigued tone, "Please clarify!" she started giggling. The cutest giggle I'd ever heard.

She walked to the edge of the pier and sat down eating her candyfloss. I sat down next to her with the popcorn and put my other arm around her. I softly nudged her, trying to move her a little back. She was sat too close to the edge of the end of the pier. I didn't want to risk her

Learn to embrace your past,
Not forget it.

falling, even though there was a railing that practically had no purpose. As we got comfortable, I explained what I had meant by calling her 'tranquil'.

"Well, on the first day of school, you wore lots of makeup, and yeah you got people's attention, but that's not you, is it?"

She laughed awkwardly with a confused expression on her face, I knew I had to explain more.

"What I mean is, getting to know you, I can tell you aren't that kind of girl. It's not a bad thing. I feel like you're someone who's more down to Earth and finds the beauty within things and in little things. You have a calm vibe to you."

She began answering, "Damn, I've never really thought of myself in that way, but yeah, I love nature, it's just wonderfully calming, and no matter what happens in life, nature is always there to nurture you, after all, we are all children of mother nature."

"I like the way you think about nature, but anyways, can you do me one favour for me, if you don't mind?" I asked

"Sure, go on," she enthusiastically said.

"Don't wear any makeup tomorrow to college, please?"

"Aha, that's okay with me but can I ask why?"

Learn to embrace your past,
Not forget it.

I answered, "Well you didn't wear any makeup today and as beautiful as you look with makeup, you look more perfect without it."

"That's fine with me," she started laughing, with a slight appreciative smile, "But all the girls you've been with always wore makeup and dressed… well… a little slutty."

I didn't know she payed attention to things like that but I wanted to help her accept herself and all her insecurities and grow to love them.

"Jazzy, do you know the difference between my exes and you?" I confidently asked.

"They were prettier?" she answered seriously.

"What the fuck!" I exclaimed annoyed but gently, "Nah, don't even Amy. Come on get up." We both stood up.

"I know it might be a little soon but I've never said this to any girl before, okay?" I started talking, letting my walls down a bit. There was a sense of vulnerability in my voice and she could sense it too

"Okay…" she curiously said.

The moonlight shone bright and the sound of the waves was the only thing we could hear. I put both my hands on her hips and pulled her closer to me.

Learn to embrace your past,
Not forget it.

"I'm falling for you," I whispered softly in her ear. "That's what makes you different love."

Before she could reply or tell me she didn't feel the same, I hugged her body tight before kissing her forehead and then her lips. As I tried to kiss her again, she pulled back. I felt a deep fear within me. I started overthinking if I was wrong, and she was like my exes.

"I'm falling for you too but…" she started speaking then paused as though she was trying to gather herself. I could tell from her shaky breaths.

"Oh God," I whispered, "That doesn't sound good." I nervously started laughing. It was the first time I'd told a girl I was genuinely falling for her; I would have been gutted if she didn't feel the same way.

"No, no I wanna be with you," she put her hands around my neck, "But I think I should tell you there's a lot you don't know about me."

I felt somewhat reassured when she told me this, but I had to make sure she was comfortable around me.

"Jaz, it's okay," I said trying to encourage her, "Come on let's sit down and you can tell me everything if you're ready, okay? Nothing you say can push me away. I like you way too much to leave, yeah. Just trust me."

Learn to embrace your past,
Not forget it.

I began getting nervous not knowing what she was going to tell me.

"Promise you won't judge me?"

"I'll never," I reassured her.

She sighed before she looked down and started talking.

"Towards the ending of last year, just before we broke up for summer and came into this year, something really bad happened between a girl from our year group, my friend Piper, and me. When that shit happened, I didn't know how to handle my feelings. I felt a lot of guilt. And well, I did something that could be seen as *unwell* by many people. I don't do it anymore, I stopped in the summer holidays, I swear!" Amy started tensing up and got agitated.

"Shh, it's okay," I said in a low voice, "Just breathe, whatever you did, it's not going to change my feelings for you, okay? I'll respect you for telling me this."

I felt bad for her, I didn't know what she'd done but I could tell it was eating her up inside.

"I think it'll be better if I show you," she turned to look into my eyes, and that's when I saw she had tears in hers. I didn't usually do well with emotional people but seeing her upset made me ache. I don't know how to

Learn to embrace your past,
Not forget it.

explain it, I didn't think there was this much to her. I held both her hands after wiping her tears.

Her voice began shaking, "It'll be better if you just do it."

"Do what?" I asked. I was starting to overthink.

"Pull up my left sleeve," she said looking down again.

"Okay…" I didn't really know what to expect.

I slowly pulled up her sleeve, I could hear her breaths intensifying by the second. Her arm was shaking.

My heart had sunk so far when I rolled up her sleeves. I pushed the sleeve back down; I wasn't sure what to do. Or what to say.

She was softly crying and trying her hardest not to show it. I put both my arms around her and lied down on the hard wooden floor of the pier and pulled her on top of me. Nothing sexual, I just hugged her tight and kept whispering, "It's okay, It's okay." Her arm was covered in scars. Self-harm scars. I don't think I can imagine what she went through that made her do this but at the time, it didn't matter.

I tried calming her down. Her head laid on my chest and I spoke softly, "It's in the past Amy, it's okay, I love you and I want you. I don't care about your past; we don't have to talk about it if you don't want to. Let's just focus

Learn to embrace your past,
Not forget it.

on the present. Let's focus on nachos!" I exclaimed in the hopes she would smile.

She let out a small laugh and then continued to say, "I'm craving nachos." We both started laughing. I hugged her again before we got up, which was a little difficult seeing as we were lying on the floor.

"Oi! You two!" a man who was probably in charge of closing the pier started yelling. "Get out of here, we're closed!"

He started to get close to us. I could've done nothing and just walked away back home, but I had to try and give Amy another adventure to help liven her night up.

I yelled back at him, "Fuck off!" and stuck my middle finger up.

"James?" Amy asked looking a little stunned. I didn't bother to answer her, the man was running towards us!

"Oh shit..." I let out worried with doses of adrenaline gathering in my veins. I grabbed Amy's hand and pulled her as I started running. She was taken aback and started screaming at me, but I didn't care. I was going to make her smile even if it was the last thing I did.

"Where are you going James?" she was yelling as we were running as fast as our legs could handle.

Learn to embrace your past,
Not forget it.

"Weren't you craving nachos love?" I answered breathlessly. I ran into one of the tents that looked like they served food and pulled Amy in with me. We hid under some of the cupboards and tables that were neatly tidied for the next weekend. When we heard footsteps retreating, I made Amy stay hidden for a few minutes to make sure the man was surely gone.

"Jammy boy, please bloody explain!" she yelled a little too loud.

I whispered back, "Number one whisper, he might still hear us. Number two, what would you like with your nachos?"

I started walking to what looked like the food preparation area in the tent and looked through the cupboards for a packet of nachos, put it in a tray, and started going through the fridge to see what I could put on top of it.

"You know what?"

"Yeah?" she replied.

"Let me surprise you," I added.

"Sure, you can't go wrong with nachos. Just make sure they're edible," she started laughing.

"Aha, I can be a good chef." I lied; I couldn't cook for shit.

Learn to embrace your past,
Not forget it.

"Weren't you the one who accidentally set the school kitchen on fire back in year 7? she asked with a smirk on her face.

"Me? Never(!), I know lots about food," I gave a smile that pretty much gave her the answer.

"Oh God, and I'm stuck with you making food(!)" she giggled.

I handed her the tray of nachos and we talked whilst eating my disgusting nachos for about an hour before I could tell she was starting to get tired.

When I realised, she was getting way too tired, I dropped her off back home and tried to comfort her about what she'd told me.

"Hey Jaz," I spoke as she headed for her door.

"Yah?"

"I know it was hard for you when you talked about your past, but I promise to try and make you feel better. I never want you to have to go back to that kind of thing, okay? You mean a lot to me and I am not leaving, so don't even try to push me away."

I tried my hardest to show her I cared. She moved away from the door and jogged to where I was standing at the porch. She hugged me before speaking quietly into my ears.

Learn to embrace your past,
Not forget it.

"Promise not to leave me, you've captured my heart already."

Her words just made me hug her tighter, I didn't want to let her go.

I answered, "I swear in the name of nachos, I won't."

She laughed before I let go of her, and we left for the night.

*Learn to embrace your past,
Not forget it.*

Chapter 6

A bullet to the heart

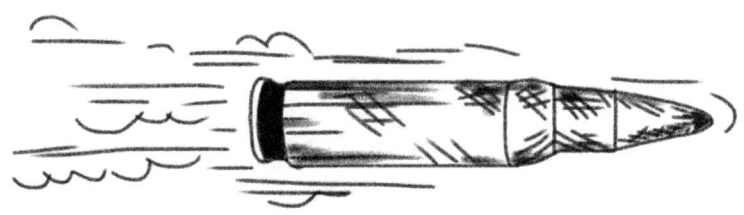

Amelia Contritum

Even love between friends can burn out,
Find a better candle darling x

I woke up Monday morning, so excited about the day. I was so thrilled by what happened on the weekend with James. I could tell things were moving fast with him, but it felt so right and divine. I felt as though I could trust him, he was the only person besides Piper that knew about my self-harm.

Even my other friends didn't know about it. I'm not sure, there was something about him that allowed me to trust him. I'm not used to trusting so easily, but he was different from all my other exes. He brought out a kind of thrill inside of me.

It seemed like what was a regular day of college and I hadn't talked to Piper in what seemed like so long, so my aim was just to make sure she was okay before all the girly gossip about James began. I went to my Biology lesson, which was just before my free period. James and I and a lot of our free lessons together so we'd just hang out.

"Hey, have you guys seen Piper?" I asked Cece, who was in the same Bio class.

"She's in the bathroom with Charlotte skiving off lesson. They're probably messing around and throwing water on each other, why?" asked Cece, again with her curiosity, but I guess she could tell that I looked kinda flustered.

I headed straight towards the bathrooms, I just had

Even love between friends can burn out,
Find a better candle darling x

to make sure everything was fine between us and just wanted to make sure that I hadn't done anything wrong since she was being undeniably distant.

"Piper?"

I couldn't see her at first but then I saw her and smiled, but she didn't smile back, and then she turned back and gave Charlotte a weird look and they both just cracked up, I could tell they were laughing at me. I felt so embarrassed, she seemed like a completely different person.

"Piper?" I repeated louder, praying inside that I'd get a better reaction.

She turned around, looked at me, and rolled her eyes, but in a way that wasn't cocky but was annoyed, like really, really annoyed. That's when it dawned on me - the little bit of hope I had of rekindling our friendship had diminished. We were hanging by a thread; I knew that and she didn't shy away from emphasising that to me every chance she got. It hurt so much to know that the one person that promised they'd stay- even they got tired of me...

I acknowledged the possibility that she could leave me ages ago because not everyone wants to carry the burden I shared with her. I can understand that she's a normal girl that has a whole life awaiting her, but

Even love between friends can burn out,
Find a better candle darling x

she meant a lot to me, so I trusted her. No, I *relied* on her. She was the only thing that kept me alive when everything happened with Ella last year.

There were so many reasons that Piper would *leave*. For starters, we were so very different. She was this person that could hide her pain and guilt. She could pretend nothing happened, but I couldn't. That's why she would leave me because I couldn't move on from the incident the same way she did.

Number two, she'd run out of things to say to me, ways to help me, advice. I'd tell her I'd cut and she would say 'okay'. Got to give it to her, at least she gave some sort of response.

I had never meant for her to feel like the only reason she had to stay friends with me, is so I didn't kill myself or worse, tell everyone what happened that day last year.

I just thought she wouldn't drift away from me considering we both had to deal with the guilt of our actions.

"Can't you tell. I'm busy!" Piper exclaimed, "So, that's what she said to me."

"Such a skank…" Charlotte continued conversing with her.

Piper effortlessly carried on ignoring me.

Even love between friends can burn out,
Find a better candle darling x

Their conversation was becoming distraught and distant. I began to have a panic attack. Piper looked at me, with not a single spec of sympathy in her eyes. They could both hear my breathing become louder, they could both see my hands shaking.

"Look, I'll catch you up later," Charlotte said to Piper. Charlotte seemed a little disturbed and confused about what to do.

Piper was fuming. I could tell she was done with me, but there was something, something inside me that had hope.

Doesn't hope just breed eternal misery?

"Listen, you bitch, can you just leave me alone?" she said in a dull tone, she had no emotion at all when she said these heart-breaking words. She was ice cold, not a single spark of warmth illuminating off of her. "I don't want anything to do with you, okay? I'm done with you, just stay away from me," she continued.

"Wh... why...?" the words just wouldn't come out of my mouth; I couldn't take it. I forced the words to come out of my mouth, I had to.

"No... No... Please Piper no!" I pleaded. The only person that knew about last year was Piper. No one else, how was I supposed to carry that guilt without talking about it to her anymore.

Even love between friends can burn out,
Find a better candle darling x

"How hard is it to bloody understand, I want to get on with my life!"

"But you promised…you fucking promised you wouldn't leave me…please… please don't," my breathing had started to become laboured; my voice had started cracking like I was almost about to collapse onto the floor crying.

"I'm just so sick of listening to your shit, *'I've cut Piper' 'Omg help me, Piper!' 'Piper, are you there?'*" she mimicked. I knew deep down inside that she wasn't wrong, she was right to leave me, but did not have to put me through hell with her heart stabbing, ruthless explanation.

She carried on saying such degrading things to me. She just kept going. And going. And it just kept getting worse. And worse. She just wouldn't stop.

"Piper, I'm so sorry, I'm begging you. I… I swear. I'll stop. Just don't leave me. P…please, you're my best friend. I trusted you with everything! D…don't fricking do this to me!"

"Here we go again. The only thing you bloody want is attention. If you want it so bad, you might as well show off your arms to everyone, and then maybe you'll realise then, it's not that no one won't help you. It's that you won't help yourself. So, stop fucking acting like there's

Even love between friends can burn out,
Find a better candle darling x

no one here for you, you fucking push people away, and then blame them for leaving."

"That's not god damn fair Piper!" my voice had stabilised a little more. "You did it. Not me. What happened to her was your fault. And I had to witness it. I STILL GET NIGHTMARES! That's where all the harm started. Don't you dare blame me!" I fought my case.

"You know what. I only did what I did because you and her were going to go to the police. Malcolm is my twin brother! Do you think I wouldn't protect my brother? You two wouldn't even reason with me that day.

I've been dealing with this shit too. At least I didn't fucking cut! I dealt with it. I moved on. All of this could've been avoided if you didn't stir shit and give her the idea of going to the police. She would have ratted out my brother! Maybe you don't understand the love between a sibling nevertheless twins, but just know, I did what I had to.

You should've stayed out of it if you were going to be so sensitive. You are a poison Amelia Contritum! You fuck up everything you go near without thinking. You have ruined lives in your past. It was your fault for even dangling the idea of going to the police. And a change of clothes and makeup will not be enough to stop you ruining people's lives in the future. My brother has potential. More potential than that bitch Ella had

Even love between friends can burn out,
Find a better candle darling x

anyways." She continued like a rehearsed speech labelled *the end*.

"I'm so sick and tired of hearing this shit, if you're not going to be able to cope with something you didn't even do then I just cannot be around you anymore, you're extremely annoying, just do everyone a favour and just go bloody end it. At least we won't have to deal with you being a whiney bitch anymore."

My heart felt like someone was physically pushing it down, and I couldn't get back up, I felt as though somebody was gutting out my stomach as I got this sharp pain in my abdomen. I had never cut for the attention of others; I'd done it to make me feel numb.

There were a few times when I'd cut for someone to notice. When Piper started giving me dead replies and would crack jokes when I told her I was going through something, I'd cut. Hoping she wouldn't see it but praying she noticed how much pain I was in. But it got worse.

She'd find out and say crazy things, or maybe right. I couldn't tell the difference anymore.

I would tell her I'd cut, and she'd reply with, *'You're still here, clearly, you didn't do it hard enough.'*

It'd bring tears to my eyes but I'd pretend I was okay with it, and would just laugh along with her forcefully.

Even love between friends can burn out,
Find a better candle darling x

But what she said then, stung more than ever.

My panic attack began to get worse.

I couldn't breathe.

My hands were shaking.

My legs were wobbling.

My chest felt heavy.

And I just couldn't take it. I wanted to die. All her spiteful words had come to an end, I was on the floor, my hands on my head, the tears had already drenched my clothes, and by the time I looked up, I saw the bathroom door close. Piper had left. Left me a broken mess. I grabbed the blade that I kept in the back of my phone case and just did a few cuts to try and numb everything she'd said.

I had to force myself to stop and not do it deeper. I didn't expect to have a relapse this bad, especially in the school bathrooms, I couldn't go back to the habit of cutting. I had to talk to someone.

I knew I needed James at that point. Only he could help me…

Even love between friends can burn out,
Find a better candle darling x

Chapter 7

Stop the game

James Bridge

Things don't always go according to plan,
With time, you'll find something better.

I had a session of p.e just before mine and Amy's free lesson. A lot of my mates and Malcolm didn't do sports. They chose more subjects like digital graphics. But I loved football and wanted to go into that profession.

I headed for practice. I walked towards the match when the rest of the team, who had already started their game, had come to a halt and the coach walked towards me as all the players stood and watched. I was confused; it was as though my being there had bought an uncanny atmosphere of death.

"James. I think we need to have a little chat mate," the coach spoke.

"Yh, sure," I said, having nothing else to reply.

The coach began walking in front of me as an indication of what he had to say, was not to be heard by anybody else. I was anxiously calm. But everything I could have possibly done wrong was going through my mind.

"Coach, is this about how I missed that penalty last week? I'm sorry I'll give it my all-in next week's game against St Mathews school."

"James," he sighed, "You won't need to give it your best next week."

"What? Why? Sir, you can't put me on the bench! I've always been your best striker," I started panicking.

Things don't always go according to plan,
With time, you'll find something better.

"I'm afraid it's a little worse than being on the bench laddie. You've been kicked off the team and this course. I'm so sorry James."

I stood perfectly still as his words echoed in my ears. My dreams of going professional had been crushed. My passion had come to an end. My whole ideal future career had become impossible. By getting kicked off the team and the course, I had no credentials in sports which meant I couldn't go-ahead to play pro. I didn't even know how to think. My mind went blank until the moment of awkward silence came to an end and the coach carried on rambling.

"You haven't come to afterschool practice in weeks and don't even get me started in how late you've been coming to these p.e lesson practices. I'm sorry but you've been way too distracted lately and word is that it's a girl."

"Coach, please…"

"Look, there's not much I can do. You've been one of our best players, but I have warned you before. We lost our last game because of the penalty and I know it happens to the best of us, but you haven't proven to me that you're on track after that. We have a big game next week. I cannot risk losing that or else the whole team can't go on to the finals. You understand that?"

Things don't always go according to plan,
With time, you'll find something better.

"Just give me one more chance, please!" I tried arguing back.

"I can't. I've gotten somebody from the bench to take your place. You don't get it James; I simply cannot risk this. Please don't make this any harder than it has to be. All you p.e lessons from now will be a free lesson for you unless you decide to change to a different subject, but you might have to choose to do an AS level or nothing at all since you're already in the second year of college. I'm sorry James."

Since everyone was watching I just took off to the main hall so I could just think about what the fuck had just happened. Everything I had ever wanted to be, came to an end because for once, I stopped messing around with girls and gave my genuine attention to one. It was a twisted morality. Breaking girls' hearts and just messing about with them, didn't make me prioritise them before my football. But the moment I stopped and took care of a girl's heart, I ended up losing my football.

I thought deeply about my different possibilities, maybe I could still try and go into sports, but it'd have to be a different subject and it'd be and AS level instead of an A-level. My other three subjects were Maths, Physics, and Chemistry, which I didn't want my life career to be based on.

Things don't always go according to plan,
With time, you'll find something better.

I was getting stressed. I had to rethink all my subject choices and I was in year 13, it was risky to change subjects. And the only person I could bloody blame was Amelia.

Yes, I liked her, but I didn't think caring about her would have me so distracted that I lost sight of something that I'd been dreaming about my whole life.

I needed to talk to her about this, but I needed to make sure I kept my cool. Anger was coursing through my veins like a poison...

Things don't always go according to plan,
With time, you'll find something better.

Chapter 8

Everyone Leaves

Amelia Contritum

When you feel the entire world is against you,
That's the point you push through the pain with all your might.

I was devastated. Piper knew the full reasons to why I had started self-harming. It was comforting to know that she was there on the day of the incident. Someone who could relate to the things I'd felt. The guilt I'd felt. But her words made me feel like I had been buried alive.

I needed James. He knew about my self-harm so I concluded that he was the best, and the only person, I could go to. At the beginning of our free lesson, I went looking for him by the fountain at the front of the school, where he usually hangs.

"Can I speak to you?" my voice shaking, a couple of tears gathered, I said. I was recovering from the panic attack I had just had.

"Amy!" he replied.

I was walking towards him a little slow, he began walking towards me too.

"Look I need to talk to you. It's really important."

He quickly understood something was wrong so he turned away from his friends and pulled me towards the school entrance. The tears in my eyes were uncontrollably getting heavier. I couldn't even see where I was walking, I was allowing his hands to guide me.

"What the heck's going on with you now? Why are you crying?" he said aggressively.

When you feel the entire world is against you,
That's the point you push through the pain with all your might.

"Why are you shouting at me, I needed to talk to you, I had a huge argument with Piper," I replied, so confused.

"You've got to be kidding me. Nah I can't even anymore" he mumbled angrily as we walked inside the building and down the corridors.

I was so scared of what he was going to do to me, was he going to hit me? He pushed me into the bathroom and locked the door. He pushed me into the wall- his eyes fuming. The anger bubbling inside him was evident, he was furious, and I didn't know why. My heart was pounding. He raised both his hands and violently placed them on my shoulders. My breathing had become shaky once again. The tears were just coming out frantically.

"What are you crying about now? You have any idea what the fuck you just did? Hmm? NO! Because you don't think about anyone but yourself! I wanted to talk to you about something. You've messed everything up! For God's sake! Nah I fully can't even with you anymore. Just fucking do it..." he paused whilst even his breaths got more and more aggressive.

"...Jump off a building, slit your wrists, jump off a chair. I don't even care anymore. What the heck do you have sad and to cry about now? You didn't even bother to ask if there was something wrong with me. I've given you my whole heart and so much more, but no. You're just

When you feel the entire world is against you,
That's the point you push through the pain with all your might.

so selfish and you're still complaining, aren't you? I've lost so much because of you!"

I didn't know how to react. Every single word was right. He was correct on every level. Piper had practically told me the same thing. It wasn't a coincidence that both of them had formed the same opinions about me, surely there was some truth behind them. All I could think about was exactly how right he was.

"You've fucked up all my chances of going into football. You've ruined all my chances of going into professional playing. Oh, my days! Oh my! You pathetic bitch."

"I'm so sorry, I didn't know. I don't even know what I did," I said choking from the tears.

He got angrier and moved a step closer. I couldn't focus properly. I didn't even know what I had to do with his football thing, but I just wanted to disappear because of how much I had upset him. He moved his left hand from my shoulder. His right hand was still on my left shoulder. I could feel the blood slowly leaking from the cuts I'd done earlier. And he didn't know that. He pushed his left hand right up against my throat. I could see the vengeance in his eyes. I was so scared. I was so scared. He tightened his grip. I tried so hard to move. I begged him as much as I could with my croaky voice.

"P.. lea..se, s... top, let...me go..."

When you feel the entire world is against you,
That's the point you push through the pain with all your might.

"Why it's not like you want to live anyways, you suicidal bitch, tell me why I shouldn't just bloody kill you now?"

His hand was getting tighter, I couldn't put my neck up anymore, I thought I was going to die at the actual hands of my boyfriend. As he tried to come even closer to me, his foot slid a little on the floor, he looked down, with both his hands still ruthlessly on me. And looked back up. He looked into my eyes.

Almost as if he felt pity. He moved his hand from my neck. It felt cold all of a sudden. I tried to move - I felt like I had to get out, I couldn't breathe, I couldn't believe it, I was having a panic attack again! And in front of the wrong person, at the wrong time. My breathing was ragged.

He still maintained eye contact, reached into my pockets, and took the blade. He blinked slowly and looked down like he was ashamed. I tried to control my breathing. He hugged me straight away. I was in so much pain physically and emotionally, and his hug was curing me. For a minute it was like all the pain and stress was slowly evaporating.

For every second that his hands were softly around me, for each second his hands were in my hair and as he kissed my forehead, I had never felt so safe. So secure. I believed there was a way out of this pain. He slowly

When you feel the entire world is against you,
That's the point you push through the pain with all your might.

let me go. He smiled, tightly, almost sympathetically. I smiled back.

"I love you so much, James. I love you with all my body, heart, and soul. And I'm sorry for everything. I'll do anything to make this right. I'm sorry I wasn't the girlfriend you wanted me to be, I promise to try and be."

"Hey, it's okay. You don't need to worry about being the girlfriend I need," he stated with seriousness to his tone

He carefully pulled my arm towards him. He pulled my sleeve and looked at the blood and scars. Then our eyes fixated on each other again.

"You don't need to worry about something that you're not anymore."

Confused, I replied, "What?"

He unclenched my fist, I looked at his hand, so unsure about what he was going to do and what was going on.

"Love,"

When he said that I felt a little calmer like I was just overthinking what he was going to do.

"You're not my girlfriend… and you can do whatever the fuck you want."

When you feel the entire world is against you,
That's the point you push through the pain with all your might.

My eyes grew wide. He put my blade back into my hand and closed my fist. I collapsed onto the floor bawling my eyes out. He was expressionless and emotionless as he left me pouring with emotion, shattered on the floor.

Too many people that meant a lot to me had told me to die that day. If they didn't want me to be alive, then who did? I felt helpless. The only thing I felt I could do, was to accept their wishes…

When you feel the entire world is against you,
That's the point you push through the pain with all your might.

Chapter 9

I have my reasons

James Bridge

Learn to control your anger,
You don't always know the full story.

I walked out of the bathroom and there was a crowd of people in the corridors. I wasn't sure how to feel about the way I had gotten so angry at Amy. I was walking to detention when I saw Malcolm. He's the one I'm closet with, no matter what he does. I'll always be strong with him. He was also in detention with me for a small joke we played on the maths teacher the week before. The teacher made us come in for detention in our free lessons instead of after school because he knew how much we valued our free periods.

I walked towards Mal, "Hey, bro, what's up. You're looking quite tense. Loosen up!" he started punching my arm in a jokey way.

"Ah. I kinda just flipped out at Amy and I feel a little bad about it. Man, I sounded so despicable and cruel," I started explaining to him.

"James, don't worry. She probably doesn't even care. But then again, I'm not the one who knows have girls will react to a little bit of playing around, if you know what I'm saying."

I did know what he was saying. He had a lot of guts to be using so much dark humour about a girl's suicide incident. It's not something we all talk about really. I then told him about the horrible shit I'd said to Amy.

"I told the girl to kill herself and..." I tried to explain.

Learn to control your anger,
You don't always know the full story.

"You did what!" he abruptly shouted, "Bro, you know what happened with Ella and she killed herself! And you've gone and told this Amelia girl to do it? Why you stupid dickhead?"

"Umm. Well. I also kinda handed her the blade too…" I said in a shameful low tone, lowering my head.

Malcolm seemed mad and scared. I could tell he was worried about me.

"Right. You absolute biscuit! Is this what you do to someone you love? This is what love looks like? If anything happens, you loved the girl and you have no idea why she'd ever end her life. Got it?"

"Yup. Got it. I'm sorry Mal," I solemnly said.

"Why you saying sorry to me you dumb shlop, people will be saying sorry to you soon. FOR YOUR LOSS! Your loss! My arse! Why on God's polluted earth did you even get so angry at her in the first place?"

"Malcolm, I've been kicked off the team man. You know how much going pro meant to me and coach even told me it was because I've been distracted lately. And my distraction? The girl I gave my heart to," I explained.

"I'm sorry about the footy thing, I know how much you've wanted that since we were kids but I'll talk to you about that later. What I still can't blooming understand

Learn to control your anger,
You don't always know the full story.

is how you flipped out at her when she didn't do this intentionally?" he questioned again.

"Well, I was so angry at Coach for kicking me off and when I went to confide in her she was sad and crying about somma. And then I saw she had freshly cut. It all just sort of piled up on me I guess and I couldn't think clearly anymore," I continued.

"She's a cutter?"

I carried on explaining, "She told me she stopped and when I saw that she'd done it again, the anger in me grew. It made me feel like even when I gave myself to someone fully, it wasn't enough. I didn't mess around with this girl like I do with every other, and seeing I couldn't help her broke me but in a fucked-up way. And now she might do something and I'm stuck in here in bloody detention. I can't believe it, I hurt the girl because of my own pain and so, I accidentally. Sort of. Kind of. Just a bit. Flipped..."

"'*Accidently*' he says. '*Sort of*' he says. '*Kind of*' he says. '*JUST A BIT*' HE SAYS!" Mal then continued with hitting me on the head several times with his maths book. It was like he was angry at me- but also worried about how I would be tied to Amy's death if she ended up taking her life.

Learn to control your anger,
You don't always know the full story.

Malcolm and I were close, I could count on him. But I couldn't count how many times he bloody hit me on the head with that foul numbered book. I hated maths, would've preferred to be hit on the head with a Chem book or somthin'.

"You done yet?" I asked in a more humorous tone than our conversation had begun with.

"No, you, dumbass. Now tell me. What was she upset about?"

I answered his questions like an interview, "She mentioned somma about a fight with your sister. I don't know, wasn't paying attention."

"YOU ZONED OFF? And then proceeded… see you got me using big words now. Yes, so you proceeded to tell this girl to die? JAMES! You're an absolute dough head, you know that? What the actual fuck were you thinking?" his hands were in his head. Mal looked the most stressed I'd ever seen him.

"You know, I don't think I've ever gotten so many insults from you Mal," I carried on fooling around.

"You think (!), You've behaved like a complete nuisance today. I have no words for you. Except this!"

I got hit on the head again.

Learn to control your anger,
You don't always know the full story.

"You're making me sound like your mother right now. But listen though, if you don't get the chance to apologise to her and well. It becomes too late; all you knew is that some crap was going on between her and her friends. She never talked to you about it much. I guess that won't be a problem since you didn't even listen to her properly in the first place. Got it? You donkey!"

"Seriously? A donkey?"

"Oh, just shut it. I've run out of insults for your clapped arse."

Malcolm and I then entered into maths, Satan's best punishment for the innocent. We didn't talk about Amy at all in detention. Everything *I knew* had already been rehearsed. I tried asking the douche of a maths teacher if I could go to the bathroom but then he started lecturing on how the detention was in the second half of our free lesson so we had a break in the first half to eat and stuff. I don't know, I couldn't concentrate. The whole time.

I couldn't stop thinking about her.

Amy.

I'd let my anger get the better of me and I didn't hurt a regular girl. But a girl who'd had a very dark past. I didn't even bother to find out what her argument with Mal's sister was about.

Learn to control your anger,
You don't always know the full story.

It clearly upset her enough to cut straight after even though she swore she'd stopped.

Malcolm was right, I loved the right girl ever so wrongly and I was sat there stuck in detention.

I prayed and begged whatever God out there that she was okay.

Learn to control your anger,
You don't always know the full story.

Chapter 10

Saviour?

Amelia Contritum

*It's okay to accept help from others,
It's what helps you grow.*

Devastated. The only word I can think of that describes how I was feeling. How could both my best friend and boyfriend leave me on the same day? How could they both break my heart more than I thought possible? I never meant any harm to anyone. I never meant to burden them; all I was trying to do was talk about how I was feeling. To rid the excruciating pain and memories that weighed my heart down. I was simply trying to survive.

Nonetheless, maybe my survival was pointless since It didn't have much value. I had to do what was best for the people I cared about; I had to try and ease their suffering if it was the last thing I did.

I held the blade forcibly, pulled up my sleeve, and washed off the blood from earlier. I switched off the tap and looked into the mirror. The tears were still gushing but I strongly felt I deserved it. I knew to end my life I had to do a vertical cut, unlike my previous horizontal ones. Doing a vertical cut was the most effective way of ensuring I'd bleed out.

I pushed the blade lightly and lifted it up so one of the corners was touching my skin and I had the other half of the blade secured in my hand. I began pushing the corner of the blade into my skin.

At first, I felt a pinprick of pain on my wrist, but I quickly started pushing the edge further and further

It's okay to accept help from others,
It's what helps you grow.

until my arm was practically shaking and my skin was ripping- separating on to two sides to provide room for a fountain of blood to start spurting out from what looked like flesh. The sink basin and floor were swiftly covered in blood. I could feel the coldness as the thick liquid dripped to my elbow and off my arm and to the ground, pattering as each drop hit either the sink or the floor.

My head was starting to get dizzy, I felt light on my feet and I was beginning to lose focus. I had to carry on. I had to finish what I started.

Adrenaline rushed through my veins as I focused my mind on what I was doing. For a moment, I allowed myself to think about what would happen after- whoever found my body really wouldn't have an easy time, I could potentially scar them- and my confidence dwindled slightly.

But all at once, the words James had said rumbled in my mind. His unfaltering anger plastered itself permanently in my thoughts. And my confidence to end of my life became more certain.

I was about to go over the cut. That was the worst part of cutting, going over cuts, it hurt like a mother... let's just say it bloody killed - pun intended. I felt ready to do it but frightened at the same time. I wanted the emotional pain to end. I wanted to die. But I didn't want to leave my family, my mum and dad. I knew this would destroy them.

It's okay to accept help from others,
It's what helps you grow.

My mind was drifting again, and I began thinking about not going over the cuts- because it wasn't too late. I could have applied pressure on the wounds, go to the hospital, got myself sorted, and survive this. But I knew finishing what I had strived to finish would put an end to not only my suffering and my guilt but rather the burden I had been to others.

Without control, I started jabbing the blade into the cut I just did, ready to haul it through my skin and harder. Ready to bleed out completely. My heart throbbed like never before. That was it, I'd done it, I achieved my goal, I thought to myself. The end.

Just as my eyes were to see the world one last time, they saw something. No...someone. Someone! I screamed inside my head as my eyes widened in disbelief.

I was immediately drawn from my lightheaded spells, which were undoubtedly caused by the loss of blood. Blood which should have continued to be lost without a stranger walking in on me. Realisation then found its way through my clouded mind; when James stormed out of the bathroom, I was so absorbed by all the crying and thoughts that I forgot the bathroom door hadn't been locked.

Oh god. Just when I was about to end it all, when I was beginning to feel the solace that came with feeling

*It's okay to accept help from others,
It's what helps you grow.*

nothing, my mind had been abruptly awoken and I was struggling to make sense of the unfurling chaos.

"Ahem!" he cleared his throat. I was standing there, blade in one hand, and blood leaking from my other. I was aghast. Astounded! I wasn't sure what to do. I knew I had to try and speak.

"I... I'm so sorry. I... thought the door wa... was locked," gobsmacked, those were the only words that stumbled out of my mouth. I was profusely alarmed, what if this person caused a scene and everyone would see, and I'd have to live with their unwelcomed judgement. Fear was racing through my veins faster than the blood. His unreactive state only fuelled my apprehension further.

Standing at the door more shocked than I was, was a guy from the same year as me, but I didn't know him. His pebble blue eyes couldn't have been more alert as he stuttered the moment he saw my arm.

"Uh... right..." his deep voice finally broke the silence.

He instantly shut the door and locked it before anyone could see this murder-like scene. His locks of blonde curly hair danced around as he moved in panic. He began pacing in the bathroom in shock. Both of us as silent as a cemetery.

By this time, I had already placed the blade down on to the counter and started applying pressure to my

It's okay to accept help from others,
It's what helps you grow.

self-inflicted wound. Until he finally stopped pacing and turned to me. Our eyes meeting in shared anxiety. Breaking the silence, he unexpectedly questioned,

"What happens now, sweetheart?"

It's okay to accept help from others,
It's what helps you grow.

Chapter 11

What is humanity?

Louis Reco

You don't need to know people well to be able to help them.
It's what helps you grow.

What the actual heck! I was only trying to use the bathroom when I saw something that'll never be erased. A girl standing there, looking as guilty as a murderer but also as vulnerable as a victim. Trying to murder her presence in the universe as a result of being a victim of this world- or at least that was the only conclusion I could instantly come up with

Without delay, I closed and locked the door. I didn't even know why she was in the male bathrooms, to begin with. I wasn't sure what to say, how to act, what to do. I paced around seeing her blood-covered arm from the corner of my eyes each step I took. The only thing that had come out of my mouth was stutters. She, however, had spoken a little more than I had, she said something about how she thought the door was locked. I didn't hear properly over her breathless sobs.

My heart broke for her. It pained me to know that she felt like such a thing was the solution to her problems. To think she'd do something like this to herself. Especially in school bathrooms? I had to help her. Mustering up the ability to form words, I asked the one question my brain could think of,

"What happens now, sweetheart?"

She tried talking but no noise would come out, she was pushing down on what I guessed was the cut she had made.

You don't need to know people well to be able to help them. It's what helps you grow.

I understood that I'd have to put my awkwardness aside and take control of the situation even though I didn't know how to.

I began slowly walking towards to her, I thought maybe that would be of some comfort. I was shocked beyond words could even fathom but my sympathy forced me to help her.

"Don't worry, I'm going to help you, okay?" I whispered to her as I approached the sink area. She nodded. I knew she wouldn't have been able to speak much at that moment considering her frantic state. I picked up the blade that was lying next to the sink, covered in blood, and threw it in the bin before she could continue what was started. Her arm was still shaking and I started talking to try and soothe her.

"Everything's going to be fine, let's clean up the wound and I'll take you to the hospital. Am I okay to do that?"

"Y...yeah" she answered in a trembling voice.

"You're 18, right?" I had to ask. Looking concerned, I realised she had gotten the wrong idea.

"No, it's because if you're 18 whatever happens at the hospital, they are not allowed to say anything your parents because well you're responsible for your health if that makes sense." She quickly understood, "Yep... I... I'm 18."

*You don't need to know people well to be able to help them.
It's what helps you grow.*

I turned the tap on and used paper towels to clean the sink area and a bit of the floor whilst she stood and tried to stop the bleeding with a bunch of tissues. I gave her my jacket to hide her arm as we left the bathroom as clean as we could do. It looked a little odd walking out of the bathroom together, but judgments didn't matter at the time- there were more important things to worry about.

Walking down the corridors was a challenging task on the account that I had to hold her upright since she was very faint. The teacher at the gate asked about where we were going. I fibbed and said we were leaving for lunch. I carefully got her to sit down in the front seat of my car before briskly getting in the car myself and driving to the hospital.

As I was driving, I couldn't help but notice she had started drifting in and out of consciousness.

"Hey, stay with me!" I yelled - half my attention on the road and the other half on her closing eyes. She didn't respond to my shouting; I couldn't think straight- If I stopped to park the car then maybe I'd be risking her life more. The water bottle in the holder sparked an idea. I wasn't sure if it'd work but I had to try.

With one hand on the steering wheel, I tried opening the bottle and when I finally did, (after what felt like forever) I held it facing her. I glanced at the road quickly to make

You don't need to know people well to be able to help them.
It's what helps you grow.

sure there wouldn't be any more accidents right before pouring half the water bottle on her face. It wasn't a very respectful thing to do to a girl I'd just met but at least her eyes had started opening. She lifted her head and started looking around.

"James I'm so sorry... Am I still alive?" she hazily asked.

"I don't know who James is, I'm Louis. And we're going to the hospital, everything's going to be fine, but I need you to stay awake. Don't close your eyes!"

"Sh...j..." mumbles continued to splutter out of her mouth, and I could tell she was close to falling asleep again. I was deeply worried that if she did fall asleep, she'd never wake up.

"Uhm...tell me your name!" I raised my voice slightly as I spoke to her in an effort to keep her from fainting.

"I...its Amelia," she answered foggily.

"Right Amelia, I'm Louis, I'm in year 13, can you remember what happened."

"I have a slit wrist...not ... a .... a concussed head", came her salty reply, which was prolonged; it would have been offensive on a usual day - but I understood the panic and other crazy emotions that were built up inside both of us at the moment.

You don't need to know people well to be able to help them.
It's what helps you grow.

"Yes well, missy, you've lost a lot of blood and you're on the verge of collapsing, forgive me if I thought you might not have remembered what had happened," I replied; my tone mirroring hers. She wasn't responding to me. I glanced at her which was getting dangerous considering my speed. She had passed out! We were a minute away from the hospital but her passing out was not a good sign.

"Amelia!" I shouted. No response. "Please, you gotta stay awake." I tried throwing water again, but her body wouldn't even flinch. I began driving faster due to her unresponsiveness. I was filled with fear, my hands were so unsteady even whilst driving.

I quickly pulled into the car park of the hospital. Unsure of what I should have done, I picked up Amelia's unconscious body, her arm hanging off. And my jacket, that she used to press down on the cut, fell to the ground. I ran into the hospital yelling to the receptionist.

"Help! Please, someone, she's just passed out and she's lost so much blood."

In a speedy rush doctors and nurses came straight away. Everything was happening so fast. I couldn't concentrate.

"She's going to be fine. Right?" my voice began quivering, I didn't know how I'd live if a girl died because

You don't need to know people well to be able to help them. It's what helps you grow.

of my delay. My thoughts deafened me - if I hadn't paced in the bathroom, if I hadn't spent time cleaning the sink we could've gotten there faster, maybe she'd have had a better chance at surviving.

Next thing I knew, tears threatened to spill from my eyes; I didn't even know Amelia, but to think my lack of speed could have been the thing to kill her was not sitting well with me.

Some people came with a stretcher. I put Amelia down with the help of the doctors. Being rushed into the ICU, Amelia looked like an empty vessel already. I mentally begged to God that I'd see her alive again. She was young and beautiful, I didn't know what happened, but she didn't deserve to die.

Flustered, stressed, scared, I sat down in the waiting area- Unsure of what could happen. The only thing to keep me company was my racing thoughts…

*You don't need to know people well to be able to help them.
It's what helps you grow.*

Chapter 12

Stitches

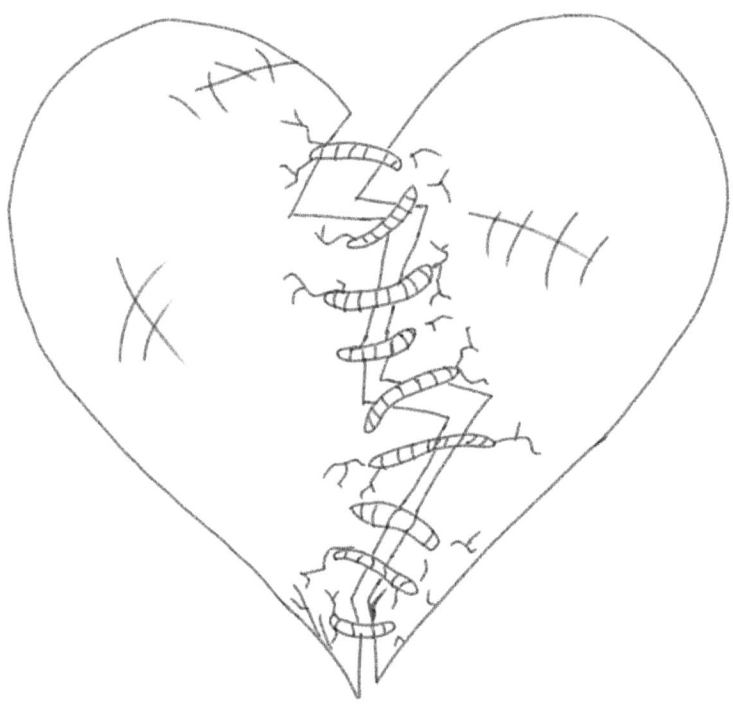

Amelia Contritum

*Scars aren't a sign of weakness,
Rather they're proof of survival.*

I woke up, my eyes unable to focus clearly. After squeezing them tightly and reopening them I realised I wasn't in my bedroom but a hospital room. I tried thinking hard to try and remember what had happened. I looked around as much as my blurry vision would allow me, and I could faintly make out two figures besides my hospital bed.

"Amelia?" a male voice spoke.

"Mm," I responded tiredly.

"I'll let you guys have some space, ring the bell or shout for help if anything happens," a woman spoke as she left the room. I gathered she was the nurse.

Trying to contain my light-headed spells, I shook my head before sitting up. As I moved my arms, I felt a sharp pain in my left arm, a pain for which I dreaded to see the cause. My arm was in too much pain to move so I knew I had to turn my head to see. I gradually turned my head, praying that my somewhat fragmented memories were just that, fragments, and far from a reality.

"Thank God you're okay!" I redirected my attention to the male figure in the room. After squeezing my eyes a few more blinks, seeing him made me realise that my memories were unfortunately correct and I was there because I tried taking my own life.

"Louis?" I asked.

Scars aren't a sign of weakness,
Rather they're proof of survival.

"Hey, you remember my name," he laughed but there was a slight undertone of pain in his laughter.

"I have a slit…"

"…Wrist and not a concussed head. Yeah, I know," he sighed before chuckling.

"Well, they gave you anesthetic when they took you in for emergency stitches and blood transfusion."

"It was that bad?" I stupidly questioned.

In relief, he replied, "I'm just so relieved you're okay, you had me so worried."

"With all respect, why didn't you just leave me alone? It's what I wanted and not to sound ungrateful, but the stitches on my arm don't magically make me want to carry on living. I'm sorry for wasting your time," I clarified.

Pulling his chair closer to the bed, he responded, "You think I care if right now you're grateful or not? At the end of the day, you're alive and well. That's all that matters."

"Physically well, maybe. But emotionally?" I asked lowering my eyes in shame.

"We can work on that."

Scars aren't a sign of weakness,
Rather they're proof of survival.

"We?" I bitterly asked. I felt naturally inclined to be a little less gullible to any guy who vowed to help me after what happened with James.

"If you're done being resentful to the person who's lost their favourite jacket somewhere in the car park because of you," he said in a cheerful tone but with a clipped smile.

"I don't remember."

"Hm, I thought you remembered everything."

I began stuttering unsure of how to reply.

"Don't worry, you'd passed out at that time. I'd be worried if you did recall that stuff," we both began laughing. "What I meant to say is, I'm not sure why you were trying to commit suicide in the first place but I'm a strong believer in fate and for some reason, I believe helping you is part of it."

"Right well the last time someone reassured they'd help me…" I defensively disagreed.

"I'm not everyone else, Amelia. I don't care about your past- I'm focused on the present. Oh, and before I forget, I used your phone to try and get your parents' number and ring them. I hope you don't mind".

Scars aren't a sign of weakness,
Rather they're proof of survival.

"What! Why?" I exclaimed. The dizziness had pretty much gone by now but if there was any left, the new revelation was enough to remove it.

"I didn't know if you were going to survive!" he began arguing back. I jumped a little due to his sudden tone even though it was understandable that he was getting a bit agitated. He saved my life and all I'd done since was complain.

"Shit, I'm sorry I didn't mean to raise my voice," he said sincerely.

"No, I should apologise. I guess I didn't think about what would happen if I miraculously survived and well, I don't know how my parents would react to having a suicidal child, but if I died…I wouldn't be there to see their reaction," I sighed out of tiredness. I felt like I was burdening someone else with my problems, "And like. I'm sorry. Like really sorry. I'm just throwing so much on you right now. You never asked for this. I don't mean to trouble you so much." I was starting to get a little uncomfortable

"Shh, you need to rest okay. Calm down, and look, I decided to help you. I could have let you have your wish come true but I wouldn't be talking to such an amazing girl, now would I? I choose my actions. And helping you is the best thing I've done and I hope you'll allow me to continue?" he asked expectantly.

Scars aren't a sign of weakness,
Rather they're proof of survival.

My mind was telling me not to fall for his foolish words of trying to help me. But my heart was telling me I had no one else and maybe with Louis's help there'd be a chance of learning to live with the troubles and guilt that chained my heart. I began considering the possibilities of allowing myself to feel emotions other than pain, allowing myself to be happy.

"Okay..." after some delay I finally agreed.

"You have no idea how good that is to hear. I promise to try and help you; I give you my word. And also, don't worry about your parents, no one answered the call, and now it's your choice if you want them to know that you're here."

I started laughing uncontrollably. Louis seemed very confused. Happily smiling, I explained, "The reason they didn't answer is that they're in a completely different country. They flew off to Egypt just two nights ago for two weeks."

"And your great memory casually forgot your parents were in a different bloody country," his laughter followed mine.

"What can I say? They travel a lot because their job doesn't require them to constantly be here, and this year I said no to all holidays because of the exams. So yeah... I forgot," still smiling, I explained.

Scars aren't a sign of weakness,
Rather they're proof of survival.

After laughing a little more at my earlier unnecessary worry (about my parents finding out I was there), he asked another question, "By the way, I never did get your second name, what is it?"

"Oh, it's Contritum. Amelia Contritum," his eyes grew in shock after I said my name. "Have you heard of me or something?" I felt a reason to ask.

Hesitantly he continued, "Ah. Nope. I just thought it rang a bell when ya said it."

He chuckled nervously.

Scars aren't a sign of weakness,
Rather they're proof of survival.

Chapter 13

Her name is what?

Louis Reco

*You never know if a person feels remorse,
Don't judge too quickly.*

CONTRITUM! I couldn't believe it. She was Amelia Contritum. Contritum! But she was so sweet. From all the girls in the school, it was her. I knew her long before chance introduced her to me. But I could never let her find out how I knew her- I vowed to help her.

She was vulnerable; not because she was right there asleep and resting after she'd tried to end her life, but because she was giving herself another chance to survive. It riled me up that I told her that her past didn't matter, I just didn't expect her past to be what I knew it was.

"What's on your mind?" she suddenly asked, starting to wake up.

"I'm thinking about your beautiful smile, think you can show me one more time?" I lied, but it made her smile wide and giggle. Seeing her even a slight bit happy was enough at the time. It was my turn to put my past behind and focus on helping this girl.

But I had to find out what was causing her suicidal behaviour. After all, you can only solve a problem when you get to the root of it and my guess was the James guy who she was murmuring about in the car on the way there.

"Can I ask a question if you don't mind?" she nodded, "Who's James?"

You never know if a person feels remorse,
Don't judge too quickly.

Getting slightly uncomfortable, she softly explained, "I guess you do deserve a brief explanation. James is now my ex-boyfriend. Before you came in and found me, I'd gotten into a fight with my best friend and when I tried talking about it to James, he got angry and that broke out into another argument, which was a little more violent than the previous with my friend. And they both told me to..." she sighed before continuing, "They both told me to kill myself but when James said it, it was the final straw and I didn't care about anything but accepting his wish. And about doing it in the school bathrooms, well that was an in the moment decision."

Everything became a lot clearer and I sympathised with Amelia. I did, but every time I saw Amelia, after hearing her surname, the only person I could think of was my sister. We were all in the same year even though my sister was the same age as Amelia. I was a year older but in their year group because I took a gap year after year 11.

"You don't have to tell me this but why do you have old scars on your arm?"

Taking a deep breath, she responded, "I'd rather not get in too much detail but after an incident happened, I felt like it was my fault and I started self-harming in the summer after year 12 to try and help myself cope. I tried stopping when I came to year 13 but I relapsed after the

You never know if a person feels remorse,
Don't judge too quickly.

fights with my friend and James. And that brings us to why we're both here," her voice began shaking as she looked down and her lips quivered.

I shouldn't have talked to her about it all so soon. It wasn't only bringing bad memories back for her, but for me too. However, I made a promise to be there for her, and I intended to honour it. She obviously felt bad about the incident, which I assumed was the same one I was thinking about.

I put my hand on top of hers- careful to make sure I didn't nudge the tubes connected to her and stroked her hand. I felt in a way hypocritical; I wanted to help her, but I couldn't deny that I had ill feelings for her after what happened with Ella.

"Don't think about them people okay. Excuse my language here but, fuck this friend of yours and James! You don't need them and they don't deserve you," I advised.

"Yes, they deserve better," she said without a doubt in her voice.

"No sweetheart, you deserve better. You might not believe me now but when you start feeling better emotionally, you'll wonder why you even bothered with these people."

"If you say so…" she sighed.

You never know if a person feels remorse,
Don't judge too quickly.

"I say so and I know so. Wait does that even make sense?" I laughed.

"Um I think so," we both began laughing.

"Do you think you'll be able to walk around a little?" I asked.

Followed with a cute smile she said, "Yes! I feel like I've not walked in so long. But where can we go?"

"Well, I heard the roof is a very remote and calming place," I joked around.

"Yes, let's go there!" she exclaimed ecstatically.

"Wait. I was kidding."

"Well I wasn't," she began getting up slowly, "And I promise not to jump off don't worry," she smiled. I was a little unnerved by her comment and worried in case she tried to do something, but she was far too weak to be able to outrun me if she tried.

I informed her on how we'd have to be very careful, "Follow my lead and don't draw too much attention. I don't think anyone should be going on the roof in the first place. Besides they were going to put you on suicide watch but I argued that I wasn't going to leave you for a second so, after much effort, they didn't formally put you down on suicide watch but the nurses have been told to keep an eye on you."

You never know if a person feels remorse,
Don't judge too quickly.

As we both stood up, she walked a little closer to me and hugged me lightly, "Thank you for all your help, truly. You've given me more hope than I had today in school."

Realising her confusion, I responded, "Um yeah, that was yesterday," I chuckled nervously.

"What! But what about school? Do they know I'm here? They can't know. How has it already been two days? What about my house? No one's home. Where are my keys?"

"Woah, calm down. For starters, I've already rung school pretending to be your uncle. I told them you're ill so you won't be coming in for the next couple of weeks. No one knows that you're here besides us two and the hospital staff. Your keys are phone and things, they were in your pocket and I've put it in your bag," I pointed to where her bag was sat in the corner of the room.

"But what about you? Are you going to go back to school?" she asked anxiously.

"I won't go this week but I will have to go next week. Can't lie to my parents more than I already am doing. They think I'm sleeping over at my mate's house for the week because of some group project. So, don't worry, I'll be right here with you for the week. Just as a friend," I reassured.

You never know if a person feels remorse,
Don't judge too quickly.

"Thank you so much, but just know one thing..." she tried to shut the door quietly behind. I made sure her IV drip didn't make too much noise as I helped in moving it as we walked.

"Yes..."

Out of breath already she resumed, "Please tell me you know the way to the roof because I sure as hell don't."

We both snickered, trying to be as quite possible since it was quite late at night and any noise would not go unnoticed.

You never know if a person feels remorse,
Don't judge too quickly.

Chapter 14
Stars from the roof

Amelia Contritum

Take a minute to breath;
And appreciate the beauty within our universe.

After sneakily walking around what seemed like a maze, Louis and I finally got to the roof. I leaned on him a lot of the way; I felt so weak but not tired enough to be able to go back to sleep.

"Are we here for stargazing?" he asked seriously.

"Damn, you read my mind. That's okay, right?"

"Of course, it is, admiring nature is calming, and besides, I think it might help you a little after what you've endured the past few days," he let go of my hand and moved the IV cord so that I could sit down more comfortably. He was so kind to me; I barely knew him, yet he was doing all of that for me.

"Why are you being so nice to me?" I questioned surprised by his genuine heart.

Looking into my eyes as we both sat down, he responded, "Believe it or not Amelia, not everyone in the world is trying to hurt you. I know you've been hurt a lot by the people in your life and yes maybe they used you, maybe they didn't, maybe their actions were not intentional. But all I want to do is help ease your emotional pain so that you allow yourself to live and do everything you are capable of doing.

You are a human being. A life. And that is sacred. I don't expect anything, and I especially don't want you to think I'm helping you because I expect something sexual."

Take a minute to breath;
And appreciate the beauty within our universe.

"I... I didn't think..." I was stunned by how he randomly bought up the sexual side to him helping me, but it was reassuring to know that he didn't see helping me as something he could sexually gain from later.

"It's okay. Nowadays you help anyone of the opposite gender, it's easy to think it's done for the wrong reasons. Besides you're beautiful, who wouldn't think that I expected something?" he explained.

I held his hand as I tried lying down on to the ground. He lied down beside me.

The whole roof was empty. It was a bit breezy but perfect. The stars shone wildly like amber stones in the sky. The moon ravished in its ability to put all the patterned city lights to shame. The wind blew ever so gently but the sound of our breaths echoed louder.

"The sky looks astounding," I muttered to myself.

"I know right, there is this poem I read once. I'm not really into poems and literature but it was eye-opening about nature."

Curious to hear the poem I asked, "Oh what's it called?"

He began laughing in response, "I don't just know the title of it, I know it by heart." He turned to look at me and I too started laughing.

Take a minute to breath;
And appreciate the beauty within our universe.

"So, you causally learned a whole poem and it wasn't even for exams?" I stifled my laugh.

"Yep and I'll prove it," he chuckled before continuing:

"Be present but never forget

Simplicity is that path to true happiness

After all, even numbness can be numbed

By simple nature is the way

Allow yourself to feel

Each drop as it drips back into the ocean

Modern days consume time within lives

But adventure that the heart desires keeps the time going

When loves comes, take the gamble

But be one with the world, and don't forget your purpose

For that will truly make you happy

The heart was made when oceans existed

Even though the brain thinks different, believes recreation

My love will always be true beauty within the galaxies"

His voice was quiet yet so soothing as he read the poem. Not only was the poem itself beautiful but he said it in such an alluring tone.

Take a minute to breath;
And appreciate the beauty within our universe.

"Woah that is eye-opening," I said.

"I know right. It's tranquil. Perfectly tranquil," he whispered. The word tranquil reminded me of the date James and I shared at the pier. I reminisced but had felt the consequences of loving James. Both emotionally and physically.

"Who's the poem by?" I asked curious about the poet.

Louis laid the blanket, which we'd stolen from the storage room, down on the both of us. "I'll let you know soon; I promise you'll get to see the poet. But for now, you should get some rest."

I leaned on his chest listening to his heartbeat, unsure if I was starting to give the wrong impression. But he didn't move me away, so I decided to try and sleep, listening to each beat of his heart like a melodic lullaby.

I woke up in the middle of the night to find Louis's arms around me. I was worried I was going to start catching feelings for him, but I took my chances of being close to him as I stayed leaning on him with my arms around him until I drifted back to sleep.

Drowsy, my eyes reopened in the morning, but the feeling of suffocation replaced my earlier feelings of freedom as I found myself surrounded by the white walls of my hospital room. I looked to find Louis on the guest bed beside me.

Take a minute to breath;
And appreciate the beauty within our universe.

"How did we get here?" I slurred.

"The janitor found us on the roof at like 5 in the morning and said he would have to tell the nurses if we didn't go down immediately."

Giggling I responded, "I asked how not why"

He chuckled, "I carried you, sweetheart."

"Yeah yeah, you carried me down a bunch of stairs and corridors and I didn't even notice?"

"You silly girl," he started laughing. I was so confused. "You didn't notice because I took your IV out. I couldn't carry you and the IV so I took it off. Hence you didn't notice."

"But how does that work?" I stupidly asked.

Nodding he continued, "When you take out the IV you get drowsy a lot of the time, IV has different impacts on everyone, mostly good but obviously when you take it off the sudden change can sometimes make you sleepy. And well you've been fed and injected so many pain killers, most of which have a drowsy side effect. That's why you didn't wake up or notice."

"You know way too much about hospital shit Louis," I smiled.

Take a minute to breath;
And appreciate the beauty within our universe.

"Believe me, the story gets worse. After I put you down on your bed, I went back up to get the IV that I'd left on the roof."

"Right…" I said unsure where the story was going.

"Yeah, so, um, well, I got locked out because I didn't realise the door locks automatically," he said speaking more quietly on each word.

"What!" I began laughing as I sat up.

"Yes! when I carried you down, that janitor had left the door open because he was sorting out some wire stuff on the roof, so I didn't realise that the door locked automatically. And well let's just say screaming from the roof for help wasn't fun."

"Oh my God!" I couldn't stop laughing at him, but I forced my wide smile to go down to a grin before apologizing, "Well I'm sorry you had to go through all of that for me. I don't understand why you wouldn't just bloody wake me up?"

"You looked peaceful sleeping?" he questioned in an attempt for an answer. We both laughed hysterically and went exploring around the hospital for the rest of the day.

Take a minute to breath;
And appreciate the beauty within our universe.

Chapter 15

I shouldn't let the past get in the way

Louis Reco

The fights within yourself are the greatest battles in life.
And appreciate the beauty within our universe.

Amelia was cleared to leave. It had been a week at the hospital although I had been going home every so often for fresh change clothes. My parents simply thought that I kept going back to my friend's house. Lying to them didn't make me feel the best way, to be honest, but if I told them where I was, I'd be spilling Amelia's private affairs and that seemed worse.

"You got everything?" I asked her as we left her hospital room.

"No, I've left my two suitcases and a tree behind," she sarcastically commented before breaking out into laughter.

"Oh yes, we'll have to ask someone to help with suitcases the size of them," I jokingly reopened the door and replied humorously. We both walked off chuckling, it was refreshing seeing her much happier than our first meeting.

After signing out at the reception, we walked to the car park. As I was just about to get into the car, one of the hospital staff came walking briskly towards me.

Confused, I asked, "Is something wrong?"

The cleaner replied, "Not really but this was near your car last week. Is it yours?" She handed back my jacket that had fallen a while ago. Amelia began laughing from inside the car. I couldn't help but smile and laugh too.

*The fights within yourself are the greatest battles in life.
And appreciate the beauty within our universe.*

"Thank you, I'd thought that jacket was pretty much gone."

"No problem, it was going to be kept in lost property but when I saw you about to leave, I thought I'd quickly get it and ask to see if it was yours. Hope you don't mind," she said as she walked off.

I got into the car and smiled at Amelia instantly.

"Nice jacket Louis," she giggled as I sat down.

"It's yours if it doesn't bring back painful memories?" I offered.

"It can remind me to stay hopeful because you never what life can throw through the door. And in this case…" she was lightly laughing before even finishing her sentence, "Who life throws through the door."

Surprised at the clever play on words I asked, "Hmm, how long have you been planning to say that?"

"About ten seconds," she smiled as I handed her my jacket. She put it on top of the dainty outfit she was given from the hospital. I reversed the car and got ready to drop Amelia off home.

"You'll be okay on your own right? Because your parents aren't here," I explained.

The fights within yourself are the greatest battles in life.
And appreciate the beauty within our universe.

"Uh sure..." her hesitant reply made me hesitant on whether I should be leaving her all alone especially since her parents weren't going to be back for another week. I considered carefully but decided it wasn't worth the risk.

"I can stay over with you until your parents come back if you'd like?" I proposed, "Only if you want me to." I was worried she could have gotten the wrong idea.

"I'd really like that if you don't mind, but I don't want you to have to lie to your parents."

"Well I wouldn't be exactly lying, would I? Like I said earlier they think I'm staying over my mate's house... your house, for a little while."

Giggling she said, "Alright Mr smart arse. How long were you waiting to say that Louis?"

"About 9 seconds," I rolled my eyes facetiously, "But anyways, would you mind if we made a slight detour to my house quickly so I can pack some clean clothes."

"Yah sure," she said as we got nearer to my house. I shut the car and got out.

"You not coming?" I asked.

Confused she asked, "What about your parents? Aren't they going to be there?"

The fights within yourself are the greatest battles in life.
And appreciate the beauty within our universe.

"Nah they're both at work during the day, and besides, if they were home, you would be treated like a fricking queen. I've not bought a girl home in some time even though there's nothing between us, you know how parents would see it?"

Realizing what I meant quickly she replied, "Oh my, believe me, my parents are the worst when I bring a guy home. Especially my dad. He acts like the boy is a prisoner ready for interrogation. Talks to them raising his eyebrows every now and then in an attempt to *'find out what they're up to'*"

I laughed, her shocked expressions and high-pitched tone displayed the perfect hilarious picture of what she was saying. Every time she'd speak, her expressions would automatically make whatever story she was saying a hundred times funnier.

Once she'd gotten comfortable around me, I saw how bubbly Amelia really could be. We both made our way to my house, but as we walked, I noticed that Amelia kept looking down.

"Are you worried someone will see you?" I asked.

"What do you mean?" she giggled nervously.

"You keep looking down. Now I'm not the most confident person but I know one thing."

The fights within yourself are the greatest battles in life.
And appreciate the beauty within our universe.

We both walked inside the house. The home scent of lavender felt somewhat euphoric after not being home in what seemed like so long.

She spoke intrepidly, "And what's that Louis. Enlighten me."

I pulled her into my living room and faced her in front of the snow-flake designed mirror.

Tittering, she said, "Why are you making me look into the mirror?" Her smile reflected intricately.

I stood behind Amelia looking at her through the mirror. Her eyes flicked up and down, unable to set on anything. Her head was lowered way too much. I lifted her chin so that she looked at her own reflection. Answering her question from earlier I said, "You're looking at the mirror so you can see exactly how gorgeous you are. Keep your head high, it's not called being arrogant. It's called valuing your worth."

Our gazes interlocked in the mirror before she turned around facing me. Amelia's honey-brown eyes glistened like shattered diamonds. A sight of enchantment that could have made even the Greek goddesses breathless.

"Permission to kiss you?" she whispered sensationally into my ear, her hand slowly grabbing my shirt and pulling me in. I contemplated whether it was wrong to kiss her considering how vulnerable she was with

The fights within yourself are the greatest battles in life. And appreciate the beauty within our universe.

everything that she'd been through and what had happened with my sister. But her soft grasp around me and her enthralling looks took control.

"No permission needed…" I carefully placed one arm around her and the other on her neck, pulling her in before kissing her sweet lips. "Your lips taste of maple syrup, "I breathed into her ear after our lips unhitched- making her giggle.

"Hope you like maple syrup then," she gently spoke as she wrapped her arms around me and hugged me loosely. I wanted to hug her tighter but reconsidered when I remembered her arm was still sore.

As I let go of her and we walked to my bedroom to pack my clothes, guilt overcame me. I wanted Amelia. So very much. But there were so many reasons I couldn't be with her.

"Damn everything is so retro," she said intrigued by everything in my bedroom. She walked around admiring all the records and the walls which were designed in number plates and old records. I started sorting my clothes as Amelia continued exploring.

"I like retro, it's a nice style," I smiled as I walked back to her and kissed her cheek, "But I like you more," I said cheesily.

The fights within yourself are the greatest battles in life. And appreciate the beauty within our universe.

She laughed before kissing my lips again, "Shall we get going?" I asked.

"Yah sure."

We left my room and walked down the corridor where she stopped to ask about one of the bedrooms.

"You have a sister?" Amelia pointed to the plaque on my sister's bedroom door which read her name, Ella.

"Uh yeah," I wasn't sure how to respond.

"What's wrong?"

Flustered by all the memories, I told her what I hadn't told many people, "My sister passed away a while back."

"Oh my. I'm so sorry. If you ever want to talk about it, I'm always here," she sympathetically offered.

"Thank you, but we don't gotta talk about this," I replied trying to stop thinking about Ella.

I held Amelia's hand as we made our way out of the house and back to the car. The more time I spent with her, the more my emotions felt stirred about everything. The whole drive to Amelia's house the only thoughts on my mind were about Ella.

Amelia's past was tainted and I wasn't sure if I could love someone who'd done the things Amelia had. And that made me feel worse about the promise I made.

The fights within yourself are the greatest battles in life.
And appreciate the beauty within our universe.

I thought hard on what to do. But when I arrived at her house and saw the way she had been brought up, my opinions on her differed and tilted. Her house looked like she was one of those girls that always got what they wanted.

Her parents were made of money, that was my immediate guess. I didn't like to judge, but the cars out on the front and the size of the house answered a lot of questions. I knew that her beauty and vulnerability was something that should have told me to be a good person and not let her parents' wealth make me think irresponsibly.

But she shouldn't have been allowed to get away with the bad things she'd done because her parents had all the money in the world. The world shouldn't work like that.

I know it sounds bad. But there was a lot that people didn't know about my past or Amelia's. The worst thing was, she didn't even know that I knew about what she did.

I was stressed - about the thoughts that were spinning in my head. About the girl I was helping. About the evil claw that had a hold on me and was adamant to make me succumb to the darkness inside me as the one thing going through my mind was,

Maybe I should have let her die...

The fights within yourself are the greatest battles in life.
And appreciate the beauty within our universe.

Chapter 16

Danger

James Bridge

*Do what you feel is right.
And appreciate the beauty within our universe.*

It had been over a week and I hadn't seen Amy since I told her to go and ...well... end her life. It was Monday again and when I didn't see her in form, my worry only increased. When everyone walked off to lessons, I caught up with Malcolm and tried asking him about Amy.

"Mal! Wait up. Right, so, I haven't seen Amy since the bathroom incident," I said anxiously.

"Shit then. Uh... Well, it shouldn't be too much to worry about. If she'd done anything we would have been told by the teachers and I'm sure there would have been talk about funerals and suicide if she did do anything. Just go to the reception and ask about her. She's probably skiving, I doubt she wants to see you," saying the last line with a grin, I too started grinning at Mal's dark humour.

"It's not funny Mal," I couldn't control my laughter. It was a serious topic but asking for advice from Mal was wise but it was like talking to a Chucky doll. The idea of the doll is serious but when Chucky laughs, you have no control over your laughter even when the doll is killing gruesomely.

"Look you carrot, we've already talked about what you should do if worse comes to worst. But for now, just find out what reception knows of her absence. And then

Do what you feel is right.
And appreciate the beauty within our universe.

buy her a nice dinner and some flowers. Actually, I don't know. Tell me what she likes," he replied.

"Well for starters you're an absolute onion!" I exclaimed humorously.

"How even?" he asked puzzled.

"You make everyone cry. Sorry, that was mostly Ella wasn't it?" I boldly spoke as we both gave each other a look where we knew it was funny but just plain horrible. What can I say? Malcolm and I made a lot of dark humoured and inappropriate jokes.

"Yeah I know I hurt her but you can't say much! You told your girlfriend to kill herself at least Ella and I weren't exclusive," he playfully fought back.

"Ah I wonder why you weren't exclusive," I laughed grimly. He hit me on the head with his books.

"Shut up, I'm trying to change now. I don't want to be that person anymore. Now tell me what kind of stuff your bird likes so I can start my path to *'redemption'*," he solemnly said.

"She likes natures. Nah she loves it. She's just totally into all of that scenery stuff. I don't mind like oceans and shit. It is pretty cool and nice to look at. She's just different from all my exes. She's down to earth and just perfect. I can't lose her when I just started falling for her."

Do what you feel is right.
And appreciate the beauty within our universe.

"Yeah, nice love story but here's what you do. Number one get her favourite food. Number two, get her... No scrap that. Make a card. Girls like that hand-crafted crap. Number three, go to her house, try and speak to her alone."

"That shouldn't be a problem. Her parents are on holiday for a few weeks, I remember her telling me," I clarified.

"Great then, dough head. You tell her you're sorry, and you say it like you mean it!" Mal hit my head with his book again.

"I do mean it! And if you hit me on the head with your book any more, I'm not gonna have a head left you sod!" I argued.

"Haha, won't be much difference there then will it? Now you take her into your car and take her to a natural place. Mountains, woods? Actually, not woods she'll think you're trying to kill her. But you hug her and explain to her about the footy stuff. And then whatever happens, well your short-circuited brain won't comprehend her reply anyways so it should be fine..."

"Great advice thanks, mate...Except for the last part you sot." I grabbed his book out of his hands and hit him before he could hit me, handed his book back, and made a run to the reception. I was going to be late for the first lesson but it didn't matter.

Do what you feel is right.
And appreciate the beauty within our universe.

"Mrs Lace?" I knocked on the reception door before walking in.

"Ah, my favourite student who loves making my life a living hell by bunking off school. What can I do for you James?" her brittle voice spoke.

"Well I know you're not really allowed to tell us this but would you just be able to tell me why my girlfriend hasn't been in. Her name is Amelia Contritum," I asked.

"James, you know that kind of information is confidential," she said to me disappointed.

"Miss please, I'm really worried. She hasn't been answering my texts for a while," I pleaded.

"It's hard to answer anyone texts when you're in hospital," she murmured.

"Wait? What! She's is in hospital!" I yelled scared about what had happened to her. I panicked about being too late in giving her my apology.

Regretting her murmurs almost instantly, Mrs Lace sighed before telling me about Amy, "Her guardian called saying she was unwell and in hospital last week and I think she's going to be resting for the rest of this week at home. That's what the man on the phone said anyways."

Do what you feel is right.
And appreciate the beauty within our universe.

"The man on the phone?" I questioned myself since I knew her parents weren't in the country and she was used to staying on her own.

"But listen, James," she continued.

"Yeah?" I tried focusing on the conversation with the receptionist again.

"Everything I've just told you about Amelia. You didn't hear it from me. Okay?"

"Okay, don't worry miss," I reassured.

"And as a way to say thanks to me, how about you come earlier. You're not in high school anymore you're in the second year of Sixths Form, next year you'll be in uni!" She tried shouting but was would never raise her tone to any students.

"Coming early? You ask *too much* of me, Mrs Lace!" I jested around. "Just kidding, I promise I'll try. Thank you so much miss."

I ran out of the reception and left the building too. I knew Mrs Lace was going to bore me with a lecture the moment I ran out of school. But it was worth it. For Amy.

I got into my car, stopped at the cinemas to buy a tray of nachos with all the dips Amy got the last time we came there and I grabbed some roses from the florists too.

Do what you feel is right.
And appreciate the beauty within our universe.

I didn't have time to make a card but I knew red roses were Amy's favourite flowers.

I drove to her house as quickly as the teetering nachos tray would let me. When I pulled up at the front of her house, I already saw another car parked there. It wasn't any of her parents' cars.

I knew which cars her parents had after the extremely long conversation with Amy's dad on one of the days I had dinner at her house. It was about a month ago, a week or two before the date at the pier. Her dad only had a lot of collectible cars because of his strong interests in vintage cars and not like the one that was at her house now.

I worried but tried to calm myself thinking of reasonable solutions like the car being from a family relative. Taking hold of the roses and nachos carefully, I made my way to her house. I rang the bell multiple times but no one answered. That's when I heard what I think was screams.

The anxiety built up - was she in the house? Was that sound a scream? Who else was in there with her? Was she in danger?

I put the roses and nachos down on top of the American red Chevy corvette, from the 1960s. I rushed over to one of the plant ornaments- the ceramic strawberry, which was painted with a serpentine detail. It contained a

---

Do what you feel is right.
And appreciate the beauty within our universe.

detachable leaf that had a spare house key. I already felt so close to Amy's family. Who else told their boyfriend of a couple of months where the spare key for the house is kept?

I walked to the door and tried putting the key in. I heard voices but that didn't help me try and get the key into the keyhole. My fingers became sweaty as I finally pulled down the handles, throwing the keys onto the table and slamming the door behind me.

I heard muffled screams.

I was petrified.

"Amelia!" I screamed.

"Are you here?!"

Do what you feel is right.
And appreciate the beauty within our universe.

Chapter 17

Getting playful?

Amelia Contritum

Remember, when people are desperate,
They'll do anything...

I was at home with Louis. I had changed from my boring hospital clothes to some of my own and I hung Louis's jacket in my cupboard as though it was a valuable royal gown.

"Hey, so what do you want to do? We can watch a movie, or I can cook if you want to eat?" I asked him.

"Come upstairs," he replied, concerned.

He didn't explain. He just went straight upstairs. I knew something was definitely up, so I switched off the TV and ran after him. I went upstairs and saw him going through my drawers.

"Louis?"

He turned around and smiled

"Are you okay honey?" I implored.

"Yeah, I just wanted to do something to surprise you."

"You're so sweet," I smiled back

"Did you need something?" pointing to my drawers I asked politely? His abrupt behaviour had made me slightly disorientated.

"Yeah, I was just looking for one of your scarves…"

Opening my last drawer, he grabbed something and turned around. Louis had one of my silk/satin scarves

Remember, when people are desperate,
They'll do anything…

hanging from his finger and a sly but sexy smile. I was turned on all right.

He came up close to me. Pushed me to the door, shutting it. Slowly kissing me, his hands began climbing up my back. He pulled my arms up and detached his lips making me want more. Then, aggressively, he tied the scarf around both my hands.

"Nice and tight," he whispered pulling the scarf to make sure it wouldn't come off. He maintained eye contact with me but smiled seductively whilst still tugging on the scarf. He carried on kissing me, taking off his clothes, and ripping off mine whilst we went over to the bed.

Pushing me on to the bed, Louis slowly climbed on top. He started kissing my neck, raising my arms again. My arm shook a little in pain as Louis used the ends of the scarf to tie me to the bed poles. I was confused about his sudden aggression when all we'd exchanged before this was soft kisses but the way his fingertips touched my skin stopped me questioning his rush.

As his hands caressed my body, I looked deep into his eyes, and slyly smiled at him. But he had a serious face on.

"Louis?" I questioned bewildered.

He got up, off of me- taking his warmth with him.

Remember, when people are desperate,
They'll do anything...

"What are you doing?" I was getting a little worried.

I tried to get up until I realised that the scarf holding me in place wasn't him getting a little *'playful'*; It was him tying me down. I couldn't think clearly because of how confused I was. I was thinking so hard about what he wanted whilst he rummaged through my drawers again.

He didn't want sex. He didn't want money, or else he would've been in my parent's room. What was he trying to do?

I was so alarmed. I had no idea what Louis was doing.

He stopped rummaging and looked at me. I was still trying to get the scarf off. I regretted the whole idea of ever getting naughty whilst having sex - I couldn't have just had sex normally? Why did he want to do this? Was I going to die? Was this a sick joke? What was he looking for and why?

"Hey!" he yelled; he got my attention that very second. "It's nice and tight..." he said in a twisted, seductive voice winking, "That's how you like it, isn't it?"

I began to beg, "Why are you doing this? Please let me go!" He ignored me like I wasn't there and continued rummaging through my drawers.

"Louis!" I screamed as he rolled his eyes.

"What?" he yelled angrily, starting to get frustrated.

Remember, when people are desperate,
They'll do anything...

"Please just tell me what you want" I cried half screaming, begging and crying.

"What I want is you fricking dead! Now stop making this harder for me…Ugh…You should have never told me your second name for fuck sake," he looked at me feeling sorry but weirdly filled with hate.

"Why! What the hell did I do to you and what's my name got to do with it?" my breathing was ragged as I kept trying to pull off the scarf that he tied with the tightest knot.

"What do you mean *'What did I do to you?'* You don't recall?"

I was so confused, but he didn't answer my question.

My whole room had been trashed, Louis had thrown my clothes out my cupboard, thrown my makeup, books, and paintbrushes all across the floor until he found it. The blade that was hidden behind my books on the shelf.

"I should've never stopped you last week, now I have to do this," he said looking at me with vengeance in his eyes.

"No… No…" I mumbled as much as my heavy head would allow me.

He came closer.

Remember, when people are desperate,
They'll do anything…

"It'll look like a simple suicide. You've got scars. The hospital would have records of you coming in for emergency stitches because you already attempted."

"Louis, I beg of you p...please. You gave me hope to live, you helped me survive, don't do this to me."

"Yeah, well what about what you did to me. Do you even know what my surname is? We shared the same surname!"

"Who! Who the hell are you on about?" I yelled.

"ELLA!"

He stopped what he was doing. I could see the veins bulging from his hands and his arms. His skin red from all the heat of running around, his eye contact entrapping me as his chest heaved heavily with every letter of her name.

"It can't be," I mumbled. His sister. It was Ella. The one I had asked about... She was the one in the whole incident with Piper and me last year. Oh my God. It all dawned on me- everything made sense.

Louis was shocked when he heard my second name. Ella probably told him about what happened with Malcolm, Piper, and me before she killed herself. That's why my name surprised him so much.

Remember, when people are desperate,
They'll do anything...

The guilt inside of me grew, but the desire to continue living and try and do good in the world also grew.

"I didn't know. Louis, I'm so sorry. I told her to go to the police, but I couldn't have done much. Piper shut both me and Ella down that day. I'm so sorry!" I pleaded as I whimpered.

"This is the only way she could ever come back to me," he softly said.

"What? She's dead Louis. She's never coming back and I'm sorry but please don't kill me for something I had a very small part in."

His delusions of his sister being able to come back to life only added to my panic - If he was mentally disturbed then talking him out of killing me would have been impossible.

Then, out of nowhere, the bell rang. It got both of our attention, we both looked at my bedroom door.

"Guess that means we have to do this fast doesn't it? But quick question." Louis spoke confidently yet starting to speed up. He quickly came up to the bed, "Have you got a suicide letter ready from your past?" His eyes were stone cold, the only expressions on his face were anger and occasional short-lasting glimpses of sympathy.

Remember, when people are desperate,
They'll do anything...

But that sympathy wasn't enough to stop him. My silence gave him the answer that he wanted to make it easier for him to convince people of this lie.

"Here we go then…" he grabbed my arm and held it firmly. My whimpers turned to screams as he placed the blade onto my awkwardly positioned arms.

I started screaming so loud, he had to cover his ears. Seeing that my screams delayed him and in the hopes, the person outside would hear me, I shrieked louder.

"Help me! Somebody, please! He's trying to kill me!"

Louis couldn't take the screaming anymore. He jabbed the blade in so hard. He did it in my right arm, the arm that I had never self-harmed on. My heart tightened and ached as it felt the constraints of my twisted life. When I wanted to die, I had survived and when I wanted to survive, the person who saved me wanted me to die.

I cried and cried, still screaming not because of the pain rather because everyone would believe it to be a suicide. But he did a horizontal cut, and he did it just above my wrist.

I prayed and had tried being hopeful that he wouldn't go over the cut and would just leave me alone. There'd be a chance of surviving. But the blood was pouring like a fountain. It went all over my bedsheets.

Remember, when people are desperate,
They'll do anything…

I yelled. I knew it was hopeless, but I wanted my screams to haunt him. I heard the front door- a shimmer of hope lit up inside of me and I hung on for dear life, literally. Louis started to panic and rush. So, he grabbed one of the pieces of my clothes that he earlier ripped off of me and stuffed it into my mouth.

I still tried screaming. Louis went on to the other side of the bed. He was going to slit the other wrist and I knew that if he did that wrist as well, even though he didn't know how to slit the veins properly, the blood loss combined would probably kill me.

I tried so hard to scream but it all came out like muffled sounds. It was going to be too late. He put the blade onto my wrist and started pressing, the blade was a little blunt, so he lifted it up so a corner of it was touching my skin (like I had done), he started dragging the blade against my skin. I cried and yelled but it simply wasn't loud enough.

"Amelia!", a voice screamed out from downstairs. I couldn't tell who it was. My parents weren't home so someone must have used the spare key. And the only person who knew about the spare key was my family and James. James! I thought to myself. If I got him to come upstairs maybe he'd be able to help me. I knew he was angry at me, but he didn't have a reason to kill me.

Remember, when people are desperate,
They'll do anything...

I yelled. Trying to get James's attention. Louis's hand was sweaty and shaking. He kept eyeing the door.

"I'm so sorry," he whispered into my ear, "But I love my sister."

"Are you here?" I heard James yell out. All I wanted to was scream, yes but the tear and saliva drenched cloth in my mouth wouldn't let me...

Remember, when people are desperate,
They'll do anything...

Chapter 18

He does care?

Amelia Contritum

Forgive people if they truly care about you.
But don't be blind to their actions...

"Amelia, you need to stop fighting. Please, I don't want to do this but I have to!" Louis could no longer look me in my blood shot, teary eyes. I couldn't speak, only muffled sounds came out of my mouth. I started losing hope.

I was getting weak-headed. I couldn't breathe. I couldn't scream. I couldn't move. All I could feel was pain and I just wanted it to stop.

"Amelia?"

My breathing stabilised slightly with the fraction of relief I felt. It was James. He didn't leave; he stayed.

"What the actual fuck is going on!" he yelled at Louis puzzled. Louis was literally caught red-handed.

"Guess I'll be able to solve two problems in one day," Louis murmured as he dropped the blade on to the floor and charged towards James resulting in both of them collapsing on to the floor.

"Louis, you bastard, get off of me!" James yelled. I knew there were many more important things to be thinking about but I wondered how James knew Louis. They both did completely different subjects and Louis only found out my connections to Ella when I told him my surname.

I tried to slow the bleeding by pushing my arm against the scarf and my other arm. I was in an awkward position but I had to try and stop the blood. I heard

Forgive people if they truly care about you.
But don't be blind to their actions...

blows and the sound of a struggle. As I bent my neck to see what was happening on the floor between Louis and James, I saw James punching Louis until there was blood on his hand. I was a little too tied up to help James out. It looked as though James was going to win but everything was happening too fast. The next thing I saw was Louis beating up the guy I originally fell deeply for. My mind had already been disorientated from what had just happened so I struggled to focus on who was brutally hitting who until they both got up and started yelling, ready, waiting for the other to attack.

"What? You thought you could hurt Amy as payback for what happened to Ella. That's between us and Malcolm, Louis! Not Amelia! How dare you bring her into this, man!"

James shouted to Louis, getting ready to attack him again. I didn't understand what was happening. Louis also wanted James dead? But what did James have to do with Ella?

As Louis pushed James into the wall, I prayed that my guess of what happened between James and Ella wasn't true. I didn't know what I'd do if it was true. I knew I played a part in her death but the only way that James would have something to do with Ella was...

Forgive people if they truly care about you.
But don't be blind to their actions...

My drifting thoughts came to an abrupt stop when I heard the sound of my canvas, which I had worked so hard on, rip.

"Believe it or not James, even Amelia was there that day. Ella would only come back if everyone from that day was gone. I didn't want to kill you, just get you away from here but if I have to kill you, then well, I'm saying sorry now."

Punching him hard, making even me flinch, James argued, "What? Are you fucking nuts? Your sister is gone! I'm sorry Louis but killing us is not going to change anything."

With the much stabbing pain, I managed to free one my arms out of the tangled mess between the scarf, my arms, and my bed poles. Using my freed arm, I got rid of the scarf until I had both my aching arms to myself.

As the argument continued, I made a decision. Louis's back was facing me and he had James cornered in the wall. I grabbed the vase for my roses that James gave me a while back, which had now died, and slowly tiptoed towards Louis. The floorboards creaked. My eyes widened in shock and disbelief. Louis had turned around

"What the..."

Before Louis could say anything else, I took the opportunity to hit him on the head with the vase as hard

Forgive people if they truly care about you.
But don't be blind to their actions...

as I could with my shaking, bloody arms. His body fell to the ground immediately.

"Damn Jaz." James looked at me in complete bewilderment.

"...Jammy? What on earth do we do now..." I looked at James in fear with my arms dripping blood, and the vase dropping on to the floor next to Louis's unconscious body.

"Amelia I'm so sorry. I came here to tell you I'm sorry," James started apologising.

"We don't have to talk about this right now James. Let's just sort out, well, this," I said pointing to the body which was lying next to our feet.

"Right, okay, I have an idea. Don't worry, I'll sort it out, but you need to go and bandage up your arms," he advised.

"How are you going to *'sort it out'*?" I asked.

"Give me the keys to his car, I'm going to park it closer to the door. Then, I'll drag him out and put him into the car. Drive the car near Mason woods and leave the car and the keys there. We won't be killing him but he'll be away from us." James explained.

His idea sounded completely ludicrous - Louis was dangerous and what would happen if he woke up whilst

Forgive people if they truly care about you.
But don't be blind to their actions...

James was driving? Besides, dropping him off by the woods? It sounded crazy but it was the only idea we had.

As we worked on the plan I rushed to the bathroom and got the first aid kit out. The burning and stinging of hydrogen peroxide pained me more than the cuts themselves. I had gotten familiar with how to tend to the wounds but this time, I vowed to myself it was the last. I wanted it to be the last time I had to disinfect my cuts. The last time I wanted to clean up my wounds. And the last time I wanted to bandage up my arm.

As I wrapped up and tucked the ending of the bandage, I rushed to my bedroom to try and erase the traces of everything that happened. James had already left the house with Louis's body and driven off.

I began pulling off my bloody bedsheets and throwing them into the wash. I cleaned my chaotic room and all the mess Louis had created. Put all the books back on the shelf, folded the clothes back into my drawers/cupboards, and threw the suicide letter I had hidden a while back last year, in the trash.

Whilst I was wiping the blood drops from my arm to the ground, James came back. As I put the vase back on to my windowsill, I heard James enter my room.

"I got you roses and nachos," he said softly.

*Forgive people if they truly care about you.
But don't be blind to their actions...*

"James! What the? We need to talk," I said astounded to his lack of focus on the bigger situation.

"Yeah I know we need to talk about everything with that prick."

He sighed putting the roses into the empty vase and handing me the nachos tray. I moved the nachos on to the table and ran towards James and hugged him tighter than ever.

"Hmm, you hugging me for the roses and nachos Jazzy?" James joked around.

"Shut up James," my voice started cracking as he hugged me back and we both fell on to the bed still holding each other.

"I'm sorry James. I'm so sorry about everything," I whispered as my tears leaked on to him.

"Shut up Amy. It was my fault. I have a lot of explaining to do. I'm just so glad you're okay. I will make it up to you. I meant it when I said to you that I was falling for you."

He kissed me on the forehead before repositioning himself so we got more comfortable.

"Jammy boy. You can explain later but please. Just hold me. And never let me go…" I said to him.

Forgive people if they truly care about you.
But don't be blind to their actions…

"I'm never letting you go again love. I promise everything will be okay. I promise to protect you. I promise to never hurt you like that again and Amelia... I swear. I love you."

His words were soothing and brought relief. It felt like taking a deep breath after not being able to breathe for so long. It was like being able to stand on top of the mountains and finally feel that huge breeze the first time after walking up the whole mountain. It was like my heart could finally beat again after being caged and trapped for so long.

"I love you too...", I whispered into his ear as we held each other tightly like our lives depended on it.

Forgive people if they truly care about you.
But don't be blind to their actions...

Chapter 19

I'm not crazy!

Louis Reco

*Romance, Friendships or even Family;
Any love can make you do crazy things.*

I woke up with a throbbing pain in the back of my head. I looked around to find myself sitting in my car- out in the woods. I couldn't think straight but I could tell it was about four or five o'clock. The sun had started to set and had the sky was lit with fiery colours. I stumbled out of the car and walked into the woods to find a bench and clear my dizzy head.

Looking at my dark, blood-stained hands, some broken memories drifted back. I remembered seeing James and then nothing. I tried thinking harder to figure out why I was with James, to begin with. The sound of the rotting wooden gates shutting as I entered the woods, resonated the sound of the door when James stormed in. Amelia...Was she still alive? I thought. Everything came back, not just the memories but the underlying feeling of guilt too.

I never wanted to kill Amelia. I didn't even know who she was until she told me her surname. Apart from that, I was starting to like her. But it didn't matter, my sister came first and she did not deserve what happened to her.

As I stumbled towards the bench, the autumn leaves brought memories of the times my sister and I used to go there as kids. We would both rush to find the bigger pile of crunchy leaves and jump on it to hear

Romance, Friendships or even Family;
Any love can make you do crazy things.

the satisfying crispiness of the brittle leaves crackling beneath our shoes.

Ella would always push me away when I found the bigger pile of leaves to jump on. I used to get so annoyed at her but they were the best times of our lives. Autumn was her favourite season. She'd always collect the ombre patterned leaves and frame them we got home. My parents and I used to tease her about it but now - she isn't even here to bring those leaves home anymore

I reached the bench after what seemed like a mile because of my perplexed mind. I was so close to getting my sister back. No one knew what they were saying because my sister was alive. And I was going to bring her home. Even if it meant I had to kill every last person that did her wrong. She was alive. I didn't care who called my belief crazy or deluded.

I scrolled through my phone to find Ella's contact. Her new one, for emergencies. And she was going to pick up because I knew for a fact, she wasn't dead. I wasn't crazy...

When I came across her number, I took a deep breath. I knew she was going to answer but I still worried about the odd chance that she wouldn't.

The phone rang. Each ring made my heart beat faster and intensified my fear. I could feel my palms begin to sweat.

Romance, Friendships or even Family;
Any love can make you do crazy things.

Hi, this is El. I can't come to the phone right now. Please leave a message and well, I'll never get back to you...

My heart sunk but her new number had her usual sarcasm in. Only I had this number, I think. Ella used a clever pun: *'never get back to you'* because she knew that everyone thought she was dead. But she wasn't.

Just as I was about to leave a message in disbelief, my phone started buzzing. It was her. It was from Ella! I knew she would answer.

"Ella?" I asked.

"Lou Lou..." she whispered.

"Oh my God. Ella, it's really you!" I was ecstatic.

"What's happened. Are you okay? Are mum and dad okay?" she questioned excessively.

"Yes, Yes. everyone is okay but I've called you about something else," I reassured.

"You shouldn't have called me Louis. I'm gone remember. I told you to only call me if there was an emergency," Ella got annoyed easily.

"But it is. Look, I almost just killed Amelia and James. I think they're still alive but they won't be expecting me to attack again so soon. I have a plan," I said.

Romance, Friendships or even Family;
Any love can make you do crazy things.

"You did what! Louis why the heck would you try and kill them?" she yelled.

"So, you can come home. So, you can be safe here. I miss you, Ella. And it's been so much worse ever since I stopped taking my pills."

"What pills are you on about? Louis, you're not making any sense."

"I was prescribed depression pills after you died. At your funeral, I made a scene and mum and dad put me in therapy for a few weeks. I stopped going when college started again and I stopped taking the pills a few weeks ago when I first met Amelia. But it's fine, I swear. I can think so much clearer now. My mind is much freer. It means I miss you abundantly though. Taking those pills clouded my memories of you. And I want you to come home, Ella. I have a plan. Please listen," I pleaded.

"Fine, but Louis - you can't kill them. You'll go to prison. Besides, they don't deserve to die!" she argued.

"Do you not remember what they did to you? They hurt you a lot Ella and now I have to live without you. No. I don't care- I'll cover my tracks. We can do it near the evening in the woods tomorrow. That way no one will be here. We can bury the bodies. We won't get caught. And Ella, you'll be able to come home," I elucidated.

Romance, Friendships or even Family;
Any love can make you do crazy things.

"Excuse me?! What the hell do you mean by We!" Ella exclaimed.

"I can't do this without you. You have to help me. You want to come home, right?" I asked.

"Of course, I do. Fine... What do you need me to do?" she agreed.

"Right, So, tomorrow I'll get Amelia and James to come to the woods."

"Which woods?"

"Mason woods, Ella. These are the only woods here in our small town. I'm going to tell them I want to make it up to them."

"For almost killing them? Louis do you have any idea how stupid that sounds? Don't say that; say something like you need to give them something as an apology. And ask them to meet you by the bench area. That way they won't suspect much because the benches are near the beginning of the woods so it won't seem odd." Ella corrected, "Tell Amelia and James to come at fourish ish and get Malcolm and Piper to come at five. Everything will be done on the same day."

"Why do you want me to call them at different times?" I asked.

Romance, Friendships or even Family;
Any love can make you do crazy things.

"Think Louis. If all four of them came at the same time, we wouldn't be able to kill everyone. There'd be four of them and two us. Come on. This was your plan and you didn't even think about the basics. I just wish there was another way for me to be safe coming home," Ella sighed.

"There isn't Ella. I've tried to get James and Malcolm both arrested for starting arson. But it didn't work."

"How did you do that?" she asked.

"On the second week of college this year, I hacked the cameras and torched the sports building on the day that Malcolm and James were supposed to lock up because they were practicing after hours. They're the only people allowed by the coach to stay behind and practice after school ends. Malcolm doesn't play but just stays with James for company. It took a lot of planning. I even got someone to plant a lighter in both their lockers."

"Yeah, I know he doesn't do sports. But what happened next?"

"It didn't work. There was a small investigation that was done to see if they were the arsonists and they even found the lighters but I didn't think carefully enough. It turned out that the lighters didn't have their fingerprints but had the fingerprints of the guy that I told to plant the lighters. But he had an alibi so the whole fire was left as a cold case."

"You did all of this for me?" Ella was shocked.

"Of course, I did. You're my sister and I'm not going to let them get away with this. I'm bringing you home because you're not dead are you, Ella. You're very much alive and stopping my pills was the best thing I've ever done. Look I love you, Ella. I miss you and mum and dad miss you too," I said.

"I'll be there tomorrow Louis. Remember you don't need to take those pills. I'm alive and well. And you'll see me soon…"

Romance, Friendships or even Family;
Any love can make you do crazy things.

Chapter 20

What she didn't know

James Bridge

Be careful love,
Anger can strip you of your morals.

It had been a few hours of Amy and I just hugging each other in bed. I wanted to stay and talk to her about all the things going right in life and the things we wanted to do together like spending our gap year travelling as soon as college finished, watching the sunsets at the beach, playing hide and seek in the world's biggest museums, bonfire nights at a rented cabin. But there was a lot of bad we needed to discuss and get out in the open first.

"Amy?" I whispered.

"Yeah..." she replied.

"I need to tell you about what happened with Louis."

I slowly moved Amy off of me and laid her down on the bed. My body felt sore after her lying on me for so long but it was worth it. I walked over to the table and gave Amelia the nachos.

"You're going to be wanting a nice distraction in my shit show of a story," I said as she sat up on the bed and I sat next to her. "That guy, Louis Reco, he's in our year group, year 13, but he's 19. He took a gap year after high school," I began explaining.

Amy smiled and replied, "Thanks for stating the obvious sherlock. He and I did talk." I smiled back at her painfully because the way I knew Louis wasn't pleasant at all.

Be careful love,
Anger can strip you of your morals.

"Right so, Louis has always hated me after what happened with his sister. I didn't think it was that bad back then," Amy looked at me worried. I didn't know what she was thinking but I sighed and continued.

"I don't care what he said Amy, you have nothing to do with him or Ella. He's trying to blame you for my mistake."

"James, what did you do?" Amy asked fidgeting and getting worried.

"It's more about what I didn't do love. It was before we broke up for summer in year 12, so before we came into year 13. Malcolm and Louis's sister, Ella, were…I don't even know what to call it. I guess they were kind of dating. They'd both grown quite close but Malcolm hadn't slept with her because Ella would always say she wasn't ready.

At first, Malcolm was okay with that, but then there was a party and word got around that Ella slept with someone at that party. There were so many rumours and pictures too, of Malcolm getting cheated on by Ella."

"I remember those rumours. But I didn't know it was her," Amy replied in shock.

"Yep, it was her. And you know what Malcolm is like right? He and his sister Piper are practically the celebrities of our sixth form and high school combined.

Be careful love,
Anger can strip you of your morals.

He was pissed after all the rumours. Now I'm not justifying what he did, but he did respect Ella's choice of waiting a while. Amy, I know for fact he did care about her but that day, his anger and pride got in the way."

"I know he raped her..." Amy mumbled.

"Yeah, he did... The day after the party I was chilling at Mal's house and Ella came over. She kept acting like she hadn't screwed a random guy the night before. Malcolm confronted her and they were fighting in the living room. I remember their last conversation like a pope remembers verses of the Bible."

"Hey, babe. You don't mind that I came over without texting, do you?" Ella said when she walked into the house.

"Why would I?" Malcolm replied sarcastically.

"Is something the matter baby?" she blatantly asked.

"How about you tell me, Ella. You go to one party without me and what the hell did you do? You fucked the first guy you saw. I'm your boyfriend, if you wanted sex why didn't you just say!" Malcolm got angry quickly.

"I don't know what you're talking about..." Ella lied

Be careful love,
Anger can strip you of your morals.

"Don't even bother with the lies, you whore. 'Oh, I'm not ready Malcolm...' Bitch I gave you my heart! I know we weren't exclusive in everyone else's eyes but I told you I loved you."

"Mal. You must have heard wrong, I swear I didn't do anything," Ella wouldn't admit to her mistake.

"Don't lie to me. it was a party you idiot; you think I didn't see people's posts about it? You were in the background shoving your tongue in God knows whose throat! Besides, everyone told me they saw you going to the bedrooms. I'm done with you Ella," Malcolm argued.

"Malcolm baby, I swear it's not true," Ella just wouldn't stop lying.

"You know what. You're coming with me! I guess you'll be ready now, won't you?" Mal got aggressive and started pulling her by her arm upstairs.

"She screamed the whole time. I could hear her cries from downstairs. She begged me to stop him but I didn't.

Amelia, she yelled my name. Yet, I still didn't do anything because it seemed like too much effort arguing

Be careful love,
Anger can strip you of your morals.

with Malcolm. I put my friendship with him before any sort of morals. I let him hurt her.

After about 15 minutes, all the noise finally stopped and Ella was running downstairs. She looked at me you know. Seconds before she left for the door, she looked at me through the glass between the corridor and the living room. You've seen the glass section of Malcolm's house, right?"

"Yeah. When you walk in through the front door, you have the walls but there are these windows to look into the living and dining rooms," Amy said.

"Yep, that's the window she looked at me through. I didn't stop Malcolm that day because he was my friend and he was coming from a place of hurt but more importantly, anger. He let his anger get the better of him. He did love her, but his love for her is what killed her. His love and anger at Ella made one heck of a poison.

I'll just never forget the way she looked at me. Her clothes half ripped, her hair messed, her mascara all leaking and smudged, her tear-filled eyes that held such a deep, burning feeling...

Five minutes after Ella had gone, Malcolm came downstairs. The other lads did end up finding out but

Be careful love,
Anger can strip you of your morals.

no one ever dared to bring up the rape incident unless it was Mal himself.

The next day when the teachers came in to tell us Ella had taken her own life, Malcolm was wrecked.

The whole summer holidays he had started using and drinking. I don't even know whose side to take. That's the worst thing. Yes, Ella cheated but she didn't deserve to get raped for it and because of that, she killed herself. Or my friend, who made the biggest mistake of his life and almost paid for it with his own life."

Amy suddenly spoke, "Wait, what do you mean almost paid for it?"

"Well, he fully crashed after she died. He felt fully responsible for Ella's death even though, I was responsible for it too. He wanted to be with her. So, one day when I was at home in the summer holidays, I got a drunken voice mail from Mal but I could hear the water in the background. I went to the pier immediately and he was there- Standing between life and death. Standing between the choice of this life and letting his body sink to the same ground where Ella's body lies to this today. Both their bodies would have lied in the oceans if I didn't make it in time.

Be careful love,
Anger can strip you of your morals.

"Mal!" I yelled from the car, which didn't reach the part of the pier where Mal was standing, "What the hell are you doing out here drunk! You could fall!"

"Ayy, James. Are you here to watch the show?", he slurred.

I jumped out of the car and ran to where he was.

"Don't stop me, James! I'm warning you. Don't come any closer. Not one step closer!" I didn't know what to do.

"Malcolm! You don't want to do this. Put the bottle down and move back. You're way too close to the edge."

"Nah James, I pushed her off the edge... I... I killed her."

"She killed herself!", I said anything I could think of to try and get him from jumping.

"James, I raped her! You have any idea how I feel now that's she's dead. Her screams haunt me. I can't sleep. I can't eat. The... way she... she... begged me...and I didn't listen to her. It's a life for a life ain't it James? Ain't it!"

The bottle of vodka smashed as both Mal and the alcohol fell to the solid wooden ground. He screamed,

Be careful love,
Anger can strip you of your morals.

cried, and yelled for Ella. I ran straight to him before he could do anything.

"It's okay Mal. It's okay. She's in a way better place now. But I can't let you do this."

"I loved her James. I loved her! I wish I never asked her about that stupid fucking party. I should've let it slide. She's gone! My baby's gone! I don't want to do this without her James. I can't do this without her. It's all my fault!" he cried.

"I pulled him for a hug. It killed me to see my best mate so broken like that. Not only was I partially the reason a girl died but then my own best mate wanted to die too. He didn't want to live without her but I didn't want to live without him.

For the rest of the summer, Malcolm was pretty much broken. Then after a while, he started using dark jokes to deal with what happened.

But all of that is partially the reason that I flipped at you that day in the bathroom. I was angry that I lost my place on the football team, but the bigger reason was that I was scared.

I was so scared that you'd end up killing yourself later on down the line - and I didn't want to be deeply in love

Be careful love,
Anger can strip you of your morals.

with you if you would have ended up committing suicide a few months or even years later.

I'm sorry, I didn't mean to hurt you, but I have a past too. You used to self-harm because of your past but Amy, I became destructive because of mine. I hurt people before they get the chance to hurt me. I'm so sorry."

"Hey, no, I never bothered to ask about your past. Okay and that's on me. What you said that day isn't your fault."

"I swear I'll never hurt you again. And I swear I'm going to stop Louis. I won't let him hurt you again because of my mistakes. He's already tried to get at me once before. He tried blaming Mal and me for the sports hall arson. But I just didn't think he'd hurt you to punish me." I told Amy.

Amy looked at me worried, "James, Louis didn't try and hurt me because of you. The incident that I told you about that day on the pier... the reason I started self-harming. That was the incident with Ella. I'm also the reason she took her own life..."

Be careful love,
Anger can strip you of your morals.

Chapter 21

What he didn't know

Amelia Contritum

Don't let your guilt control you,
Talk to people who can genuinely help you.

"How can you even be involved with what happened with Ella?" James asked curiously.

"It was the same day Malcolm raped Ella. It was getting to the end of the school year so Piper and I would just hang out a lot more even if there was college the next day.

We were both walking back from college to her house. We were planning to have a sleepover and burn down her house with our terrible baking skills. But we were sat outside on the bench for a while. Do you know which bench I'm talking about?"

James replied, "Yeah, it's the bench on their street. About two minutes away from their house."

"That's the one. I even remember what we were talking about that day. Piper and I were debating about which is the better cake, Chocolate, or Victoria Sponge.

Anyways, just randomly whilst we were talking, we saw a girl. She was staggering with every step she took. She could barely walk and looked as though she couldn't breathe either. I realised she was from our year group. Ella Reco. And well I didn't know her very well but Piper knew that Ella was Malcolm's girlfriend.

Her eyes were fear-stricken when she looked towards us. Logically, we were confused as to what had happened

Don't let your guilt control you,
Talk to people who can genuinely help you.

and we convinced her to talk to us about what was going on.

"Ella? Oh my God, are you okay? What's going on?" were the first things I asked. Piper had the same questions in mind.

Half choking on her own tears, she replied, "He... he... he..." She was weeping and whimpering. At the time piper and I couldn't understand what happened and pressed her to explain.

Piper, in her attempt to be communicative, whispered, "It's okay Ella. Just tell us what happened. Is someone hurt in there?" She pointed to her house with her finger starting to look tenser than she had been earlier.

Ella began talking in a slightly calmer way than she had begun but the tears were gathering in her eyes and she wouldn't dare to be touched by either me or Piper. Even a hand on her shoulder for reassurance made her agitated.

"It was... your brother... M...Malcolm..."

"What did he do Ella? You have to tell us!" Piper was growing impatient and it didn't make Ella's fear lessen.

I gave Piper a concerned look to hint that she should be asking Ella with a bit more composure and kindness.

Don't let your guilt control you,
Talk to people who can genuinely help you.

I gave Ella a sympathetic smile in an attempt to calm her nerves, "It's okay, we're right here, nothing bad is going to happen. Now just tell us, what has happened so we know whether or not to call an ambulance."

"An ambulance!" Both Ella and Piper and exclaimed in sync.

"Yes," I began explaining, "If somebody's hurt in that house or someone broke into the house, we need to call someone."

Piper was getting worried and I could tell she was contemplating on just ditching us and running to the house to see what had happened. But Ella had been worked up by my suggestion of an ambulance and finally spat out what happened.

"He raped me!"

"James, my heart immediately sunk that day. A heartache took over my whole body and I felt sick to my stomach. I didn't want to believe something as awful as that happened. Words wouldn't even come out of my mouth because of the shock."

"Malcolm stripped me naked and did what he desired with me. As though I wasn't even a person but just an

Don't let your guilt control you,
Talk to people who can genuinely help you.

ob...object. I begged him! I cried and screamed. B...but he didn't even stop!" Ella's painful explanation was too graphic for me. My eyes got teary just listening to her talk about it. But Piper was stood there, stone cold. It was obvious she was shocked, but it was as though she was fighting some part of her to not show any emotions.

"You have to tell someone Ella. You have to go to the police," I advised

"But what... if...if he tries to hurt me if I go to the police," She kept crying.

"Ella! He's already hurt you!" I expressed.

Piper suddenly spoke, "No. if you go to the police, then I'll hurt you myself!"

"Piper, what the heck are you on about?" I asked confusedly.

"Amelia stay out of this. Ella, I'm sorry about what my brother did to you, but I can't let you go to the police," Piper said sternly.

"I don't want to see him ever again. I'm sorry... b...but I'm going to the police," Ella stuttered.

"No, you're fucking not!" Piper got aggressive about the situation quickly and Ella was getting more alarmed by the second. "You think a guy would ever dare to go

Don't let your guilt control you,
Talk to people who can genuinely help you.

after the girlfriend of my brother, Malcolm Jackson. Honey, we run the school. That guy at the party, he was told to try and fuck you."

"Piper what did you do?" I asked looking at my best friend and seeing a completely different person.

"It's simple. Malcolm is practically perfect. Every girl wants him; he's got everything a girl wants. Good looks, our parents are rich as hell and he's practically the most popular guy in college. So, when he told me that Ella wanted to wait to have sex, well, I had to test it out." At this point, Ella's face had dropped and I was shocked at what Piper had done.

But she had the same emotionless expression as she continued explaining, "I paid a guy to try and sleep with you at that party to see if you genuinely weren't ready for sex or if you were just playing with Malcolm's heart for money. And well the guy you slept with, I told him to have cameras set up in that room. I was going to leak the footage if you didn't break up with him, but I guess Malcolm did that himself.

"Why?... Why... would you do that?" Ella cried and I stood there not knowing what to do. I was standing there watching my best friend threaten a girl who had just been raped. My best friend whom I cared about so much had done such horrible things to protect her family's rich pride and reputation.

Don't let your guilt control you,
Talk to people who can genuinely help you.

"Because I wasn't going to let some random whore come into my house and ruin my brother's reputation. It was better if you left now rather than later. I care about my brother. Always will. So, if you go to the police. That tape of you fucking the guy from the party… well. How's it going to look for the girl that cheated on Malcolm Jackson- the guy that even the teachers respect."

"Piper, don't, she's been raped!" I yelled at her. But Piper didn't listen and Ella ran off, more hurt than before and in an inescapable conflict.

"That's the last time I ever talked to Ella. I regret not running after her and taking her to the police station myself - or not trying hard enough to stop Piper's threats.

So that's what happened James. You and Malcolm aren't the reason that Ella killed herself. Piper trapped her with threats and I didn't do anything. I could've tried helping Ella or tried getting rid of the tape but I didn't and the next day, when we were told Ella had jumped off the pier, I felt like it was my fault.

The guilt got way too much. So, I started self-harming as a way to punish myself for not doing more that day.

Don't let your guilt control you,
Talk to people who can genuinely help you.

But Piper was fine with a girl dying if it kept her brother from prison and if it kept her popularity stable.

I kept trying to talk to her about the guilt I felt. But our friendship started decaying and the fight she and I had, well it was regarding what happened that day with Ella.

She was getting sick and tired about how I changed and would self-harm after the incident so she told me to just end my life too."

"Shit Amy... and I told you to kill yourself straight after. Amelia. I'm so sorry," James apologised.

"No, it's my fault for not coping with my guilt a better way," I tried comforting him.

"Amy?"

"I'm being serious James, it's truly okay."

Shocked, he said, "No, it's not that. But it's Louis...he just texted..."

Don't let your guilt control you,
Talk to people who can genuinely help you.

Chapter 22

It's four - one

James Bridge

*Your actions can change a person's life forever,
Think carefully x*

"What! What do you mean Louis texted you?" Amy asked astounded.

"I don't know, I just looked at my phone and saw a notification from him," I answered equally confused.

"What did he say?"

"James, look, I want to apologise for what I did. I now understand my sister took her own life and it's not your guys' fault. Please just come to the clearing of Mason woods at 4oclock tomorrow. Bring Amelia with you. I need to give you guys something. It's to do with Ella."

Amy and I looked at each other, unsure and stunned at the message.

"What the actual fuck..." I said.

"Do you think he's being serious?" Amy asked - starting to stress eat her nachos.

"He wouldn't dare try anything with us after what he did today. It wouldn't make sense to try and get rid of us again so soon. Maybe he genuinely wants to give us something," I contemplated.

"I don't think we should go," Amy was assertive in her decision. "No one just simply *'realises'* that their sister's suicide wasn't our fault and wants to apologise after trying to kill us. Besides, why apologise in the woods? He can say sorry in a public place, or better yet, over text?"

Your actions can change a person's life forever,
Think carefully x

I could tell Amy was scared and cautious about seeing Louis again. It made sense that she was going to think the worst of him after he practically gained her trust, kept the truth about being Ella's brother from her, and then tried to kill her.

"Look Jaz, don't worry. There's two of us and one of him. We'll be fine. You don't have to come; I'll go myself and bring back whatever he wants to give. And I won't forget about what he did today, I'll be cautious. And I think he lives near the woods - that's why he probably called us there. It's probably just convenient to meet there," I assured her.

"Fine, but I'm coming with you. I'm not going to let you go alone like you said; it'll be harder for him to try and do anything if there's two of us and one of him. Now, can we go downstairs? I want to check something."

"Sure. What is it?" I asked as we walked down the stairs simultaneously.

"He left his bag here. I want to see if he brought something from home to kill me."

"Wait, he was staying here?" I was confused as to why Louis's things were at Amy's house.

"Well, he was going to. He found me in the bathroom after I tried ending it and took me hospital. He stayed with me the whole week there and then I asked him to

Your actions can change a person's life forever,
Think carefully x

stay this week at mine because I wasn't planning to go into college this week either."

I couldn't blame her. She was in the hospital because of what I said and in a way I'm grateful Louis saved her and took care of her even though he tried doing the opposite subsequently.

We went into the living room and put Louis's bag onto the table.

"Are you sure you want to do this?" I asked, worried that the contents of the bag would upset her more.

"Yes. If there's something like a knife inside, it meant the whole time he was planning to kill me. But if not, then maybe... he decided in the moment and it'll be easier to forgive him for that," she sighed.

"Forgive him? You don't need to!" I was surprised that Amy thought it was necessary to forgive someone who almost murdered her.

"James, Louis and I kissed... and the reason half my clothes were off when you came in was because we were about to well... you know. And I didn't love him, but I did like him. I pray that there's nothing like that in his bag, not because I liked him, but because it would mean he was deceiving me the entire time. And that, I won't stand for."

Your actions can change a person's life forever,
Think carefully x

I was a little upset that Amy had kissed another guy but, in her defence, we weren't even together at the time. And I knew better than to let her go again. I was going to do everything I could to cherish every moment with her because she had a special place in my heart – like no other girl. Yes, she was a little bit complicated, but that's what made her different.

Amy continued, "Hey, don't worry. Whatever's in that bag, it doesn't matter. I love you and I want you. I liked him but I loved and love you. I know our love isn't perfect James. It hasn't had the best start, especially since we didn't know a big part of each other's lives. But weirdly, you're a part of my heart."

"Ugh, Jaz, you're really building up the tension of what's in the bag," I smiled at her before hugging her.

She giggled, "I'm not done yet Jammy boy.

Your name is engraved in my heart darling. You make me the happiest I've ever been. We were together for like a few months but I feel like I've been with you for much longer. You gave me so many adventures in such a short time, I can't even think about how many other pier workers you're willing to piss off and then run away from.

Point is you make me smile until my bloody cheeks hurt. You make me feel protected in your arms. You make me

Your actions can change a person's life forever,
Think carefully x

happy. Darling, I love you and I never want to lose you," she hugged me tighter than I thought possible.

"Would you still love me if I took you back to that haunted house from our first date and ditched you there?" I asked teasingly.

"Nah then I'd kill you before Louis ever could," we both laughed hard and decided to open the bag in a happier spirit. There was no knife, just clothes, and a book but there was something else.

A bottle of pills.

"What are these for?" I asked Amy in the assumption she would know.

"God knows. I've never seen him take any tablets, besides it's unopened. Look." The bottle was as sealed as a vault.

I didn't understand, "Did he get them from the pharmacy today or something?"

"No. I was with him the whole time. Does it say what the pills are for?"

I turned the bottle of pills around to see the label had been ripped off and there was no way of knowing what the tablets are for.

"No, it's been ripped off. Amelia?" I had a theory…

Your actions can change a person's life forever,
Think carefully x

"Yes, James?" Amy responded confused.

"Hear me out. What if the reason he thinks his sister is alive and all that crap about killing us will bring her back alive... what if that's because he's not been taking his pills?" I considered.

"That would make sense, but why all of a sudden now... Oh," Amy murmured.

"Oh?" I repeated.

"Right. Well, Louis hadn't tried anything the whole week but today when we were at his house and I asked about his sister. He told me she died. At the time I didn't know that Ella and Louis were siblings because I never asked for his surname. But maybe bringing up his sister just triggered him."

"Maybe," I mumbled as I tried to make sense of the whole situation.

The sudden silence then filled with my ringtone as my phone rang. It was Malcolm, he probably wanted to know about Amy.

"James?" Malcolm sounded concerned over the phone.

"Yeah, Mal. Don't worry everything went fine with Amy," I replied. Amy gave me a small smile since she gathered, I'd told Malcolm about our relationship.

Your actions can change a person's life forever,
Think carefully x

"Yeah, that's great and all. But we have a problem. You need to come over and I think you should bring Amelia too. Now!" Malcolm continued.

I put the phone down at once.

"Amy, we got to go!" I yelled as I ran for my car. She didn't ask any questions and followed me straight away.

I waited for Amy to lock the house door and come inside the car before pushing my foot on the gas.

"James. What's wrong!" Amy yelled over the loud sound of the car's engine.

"I'm not sure. Malcolm said we need to go over right now. He sounded stressed."

I kept thinking about what the emergency could be the whole way. His house wasn't far from Amy's, I pulled into the driveway and got out of the car. We rang the doorbell and both Malcolm and Piper were by the door waiting for us.

"You're going to want to hear this James," Mal said as he walked towards the dining room.

"This better be important. Amy and I had a bit of a rough encounter with Louis today and we're trying to sort somma out," I warned in the thoughts that Mal had overreacted on the phone.

Your actions can change a person's life forever,
Think carefully x

"That's exactly why I called you," Malcolm said as he sat down at the fancy marbled dining table.

"We got a text from him. Both of us," Piper intervened.

I walked up from the table and went to the cupboards to grab some glasses before pouring some Bourbon

Amy drank her cup in one sip before saying, "We got a text too."

"Telling you to meet him at five?" Malcolm asked.

I replied, "No, he said four to us…"

"We shouldn't go. There's something not right. Why would he want to apologise to them?" Amy announced.

Malcolm and Piper looked stunned at Amy's comment but I explained to stop their confusion, "Louis just tried to kill me and Amy. Literally a few hours ago. That's why we thought his texted about apologising."

"What!" Piper and Mal shouted in sync.

"Why did he do that?", "Did you say kill?", "He's never tried that before.", "Why didn't you call the police?" - I couldn't even tell who was asking the questions as the commotion rose and I took another drink.

"He's pissed off about his sister. What do you think!" I yelled as everyone went silent.

Your actions can change a person's life forever,
Think carefully x

"Look, Piper, did you tell Malcolm about how you saw Ella that day?" I asked.

Malcolm replied instead, "Yeah, I know about it all. Piper told me a while back. But it's not even Amy's and Piper's fault. It's not yours either James. It's mine, and Louis needs to back off. This is getting crazy. First arson and now he tried to kill you?"

"How about we just go and see what the hell he wants?" Piper proposed.

"He's given you guys a different time to us. There's something completely not right about this," Malcolm said worriedly.

"Well, why don't we all just go at once then. We'll go at the earliest time, four, and well, what's he going to do? Ask us to come back at a different time(!) With all respect, that guy doesn't get much flexibility when he wants to talk to us," Piper was being blunt about her thoughts to the whole situation.

We all looked at each other hesitant about whether we should agree.

I stepped in since what Piper was saying made sense, "It'll be four of us and one of him. We have a chance to move on from this fucking disaster now. And it's like I was saying to Amy earlier, maybe he genuinely needs to give us something,"

Your actions can change a person's life forever,
Think carefully x

Everyone nodded and the plan was determined. We were all going to ride together and meet Louis at four to sort our many issues out.

"Now that that's decided. Are you guys going to be staying the night here? Our parents won't mind and well there's plenty of spare rooms. Or you could just share," Malcolm winked at me and Amy. She gave her awkward laugh like she does when she doesn't know what to say.

She pinched me from underneath the table and I quickly realised that Piper and Amy were still on rough terms. It would have been uncomfortable for her if we stayed there.

"Nah, we still got to finish up cleaning Amy's house since Louis trashed it," I tried using as an excuse. "But we'll pick you up tomorrow at half three here."

"Yep. If anything happens let us know yeah?" Malcolm said before walking with us to the house door and seeing me and Amy off.

We grabbed takeaway and went back to her house to get everything ready for the night. We double-locked the main doors and shut the blinds and windows but kept a small light on in the passage before going up to her bedroom.

Your actions can change a person's life forever,
Think carefully x

As Amelia got changed and I took off my shirt (since I had no other clothes to change in to), I noticed her struggling to change her bandages.

"Do you want me to do it instead?" I offered.

"Yeah, please. I'm right-handed and he did it on my right arm so now it's a little bit weird using my left arm to try and clean everything up," she let out an awkward chuckle.

I walked over to her dressing table which had her textbooks in a neat stack and stationery organised perfectly in a row. I opened the first aid kit which also sat neatly on the table and picked up an antibacterial wipe.

Her left arm had already been bandaged up by the hospital and didn't need to be redone until she was ready to take it off. But her right arm, where Louis had hurt her, kept bleeding through the bandage.

I unravelled the bloody bandage and saw what he did to her. Her skin sliced and bruised up from being tied up so roughly. It was hard seeing her trying to be strong even though I could tell she was starting to get teary. I opened the antibacterial wipe and cleaned the extra blood. Her arm was trembling each time the wipe touched the wound.

*Your actions can change a person's life forever,
Think carefully x*

What made it worse was knowing I could have stopped this but I never did think about the consequences. I finished wiping the wound and wrapped a new bandage.

I looked at Amy in her watering eyes. She kept trying to look everywhere but at me.

"It's okay Jammy boy..." she tried letting out a smile. "I'm fine," she lied.

I didn't reply. I just hugged her.

It was at that moment when I finally understood why Malcolm wanted to jump off that day. I can't even describe how much I loved her and she made me want to be a better person. Especially for her. I knew to never put her in a situation where I could lose her again. My name may have been engraved in her heart but her name burned through mine.

I would have given my life for Amelia...

Your actions can change a person's life forever,
Think carefully x

Chapter 23
Clearing of the woods

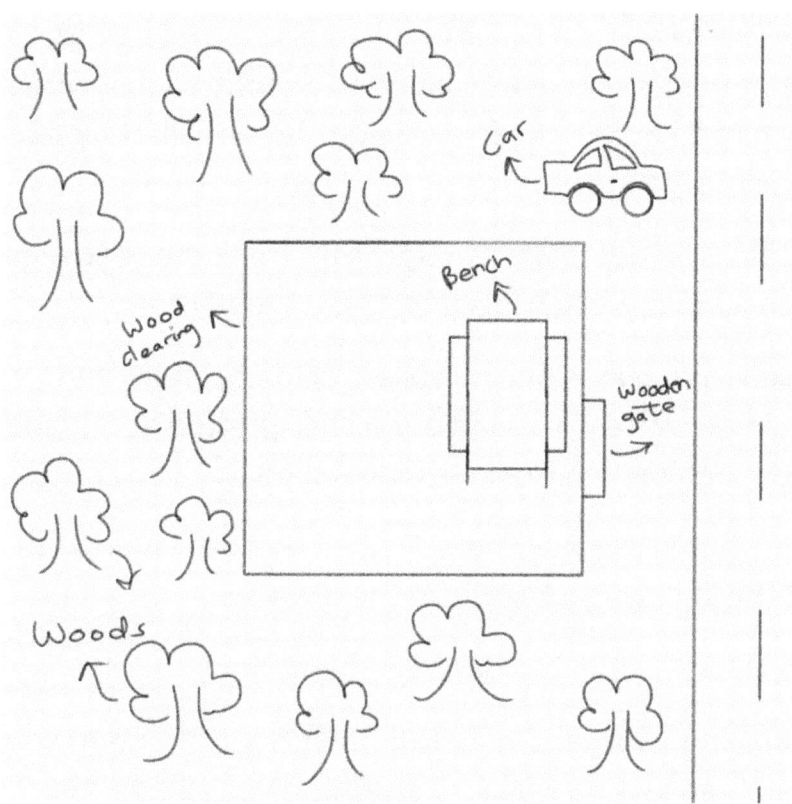

Amelia Contritum

Don't forget,
We are not eternal...

I woke up late to find James wasn't in the bed. It was already noon. I went to the bathroom before going downstairs to see where James had gone.

"James?" I called out as I checked all the rooms downstairs.

"In here!" I heard from the kitchen.

And there he was, shirtless but wearing a hilarious banana print apron I forgot we had.

"What the actual fuck!" I laughed uncontrollably when I saw him. I couldn't keep a straight face at all. He looked ridiculously funny.

"What? You don't like my clothes? I think the yellow goes nicely with my black joggers," he witted around.

Deciding to play along, I replied, "No no, I think red would go better." I pulled out a chilli printed apron and held it against me like I was modelling it.

"Ooh. Looking spicy there Jazzy," we both laughed as I put the chili apron back into the drawers.

"So, what ya cooking darling?" I asked.

"Anything you want love. But. Quick question…do you think I can just do the easy stuff and you can do the actual cooking?" he looked down at the hob which he

Don't forget,
We are not eternal…

was struggling to turn on and then looked back at me worried.

"Well, Mr *'can't cook at all'*. How about you take that apron off and leave it to me," I giggled and James still stood there not having a single clue about what to do with the pan in his hands.

"Aw shit, you don't like me in an apron?" he chuckled.

"Nah I prefer you shirtless… and without this ridiculous apron!" I laughed as I tried taking off his apron.

"Hey no! I'm ticklish!" I squealed as James tickled me to stop me from taking off the apron.

We fooled around the whole time we made breakfast and got ready. I added finishing touches to my jewellery and changed into a long-sleeved crop top.

"You look beautiful," James randomly said whilst standing by my bedroom door, admiring the way I did my makeup and put my jewellery on.

"Guess what. I'm barely wearing makeup," I said in remembrance to one of our dates when he told me that I should stick to natural makeup.

"And you look perfect without it…" he came towards me and kissed me before twirling me around in the air and hugging me. His skin was as warm as a hot cup of cocoa

*Don't forget,
We are not eternal…*

and his hands didn't just hold me tight, they held my hope for a happy life with him tight.

"Are you going to go over to Malcolm's house shirtless?" I asked half laughing and confused as to why he wasn't ready.

He looked at me smiling and chuckled, "Shall I put the banana print apron back on? Just kidding. I don't have any clothes here so I'll just borrow a shirt from Mal when we get there. And you know what that means?"

"Enlighten me," I said intrigued.

"It'll mean you get a nice view the whole car ride there," he winked at me.

"Yeah, you're right. There's a lot of scenic stuff on the way to their house," I slyly responded.

"Damn Jaz. That spice is starting to kick in isn't it?" he joked as we departed for the car.

I giggled but was very consumed with anxious thoughts about the day. James seemed pretty calm the whole car ride, but if what James had theorised earlier about Louis not taking his pills was correct, then we would have been:

- Walking into a remote location,
- To a someone who hasn't taken their pills,

Don't forget,
We are not eternal...

- Who has attempted to kill us,
- And has a desire for vengeance.

We were striding into the face of death, unarmed, and with an optimistic view even though the whole idea of meeting up with Louis was hellish. And there's nothing optimistic about hell.

We pulled up to their house and Piper and Malcolm were waiting out the door for us.

"We ready to go?" James asked when everyone got into the car.

"Why the bloody heck are you shirtless you turnip!" Malcolm laughed in surprise.

"Oh yeah, I forgot about that. I didn't have any clothes at Amy's and didn't want to wear the same shirt. I was gonna ask to borrow one of yours." James chuckled and started driving.

"So why are you driving off?" Piper asked.

"Oh yeah. I don't know..." James replied. The atmosphere and tension lightened and everyone started laughing at James's dopiness.

"Bro just leave it. Go shirtless," Malcolm said.

"But its fricking freezing!" James whined.

Don't forget,
We are not eternal...

"So why are you still driving ahead!" I laughed at James's indecisiveness.

"I don't know. Ugh, it's fine Imma just go shirtless, but we're not staying there long. No more than half an hour. And it's not like it takes very long to say sorry and give something, does it?" he said unworried about meeting Louis.

Piper stepped in to ask the question everyone had been thinking, "What do you think he wants to give?" everyone went silent in their lack of answers.

"Hopefully the name to the pills he should be bloody taking," James replied sceptically.

"What's that about?" Malcolm asked

I answered, "Louis left his bag at mine and when James and I opened it, we found a bottle of unopened pills. He'd never taken them before in front of me but the label was ripped off. James thinks he had a bit of a psychotic breakdown and thinks his sister is alive because he hasn't been taken his pills. But we can't be sure of that if we don't know what the pills are for. For all we know, they could be prescribed painkillers."

"What!" Malcolm yelled suddenly, "James, going there is not a good idea. You guys are telling me just now that he's not been taking his pills and tries to kill you guys but then wants to meet up to apologise!

Don't forget,
We are not eternal...

What, are you fucking crazy?! I'm sorry but turn the car back around, we can't go there!"

Malcolm's nervousness calmed me down. It was soothing knowing I wasn't the only person who thought going to the woods to meet Louis was completely absurd.

"No. James, keep on driving," Piper argued whilst James sighed in stress, "Look Mal, we're already here. Let's see what he wants. There's four of us remember. For once can you guys just put your bloody guilt aside and look at the incident for what it was! Suicide. She chose to do it, and the sooner you lot and Louis see it as just that, the quicker we can move on from this bullshit."

I knew Piper's little lecture was aimed very much at me but I didn't want to cause another argument. Piper was ruthless when she wanted something and there was no use fighting back with someone like her. They argued about going to do the woods the whole ride.

"Right. We're here," James said as he parked the car on the pavement close to the gate of the woods. It was the first time I saw James talking in so much distress. But listening to Malcolm and Piper's argument was enough to get anyone worked up.

Malcolm was in a childish strop but he finally agreed and everyone got out of the car.

Don't forget,
We are not eternal...

We walked through the manky wooden gate that took us past a small section of trees and then into the clearing of the woods where a plain double bench sat. And Louis was sat there. Waiting for us.

"Why are you all here?" he said astounded and got up immediately. I held James's hand the moment Louis got closer to us. I was terrified of what was going to happen -What if someone got hurt? What if James got hurt?

Malcolm took the opportunity to reply cockily, "Well, you wanted to give us all something. We just thought it'd be easier if we came here at once. Didn't want to waste too much of your time(!)"

Louis was gob-smacked and looked confused on what to do, "And why is he shirtless?", he continued even more confused.

"Come on Louis, it shouldn't really be a problem that we're all here. Unless you had something planned? And can we just not talk about the shirt? It's complicated," James replied and began walking towards Louis. I pulled him back in fear that James was going to start a fight.

Looking at my hands that held James's, Louis commented, "Wow Amelia. So, you're back together with the guy that told you to kill yourself. Don't you remember how broken you were before I came along?

Don't forget,
We are not eternal...

But I guess you deserved all of that for what you did to my sister. I should've never taken you to the hospital."

"Leave her out of this. What happened with your sister wasn't her fault but mine. I don't know what Ella told you before she killed herself but Amelia barely said anything that day. But it was me who threatened Ella," Piper spoke up. I felt like the rigidity between me and Piper smoothened when she said that. For once I felt like I wasn't completely alone. I had my boyfriend and my best friend who cared about me.

"She's still alive! You guys just drove her out of town. She's going to come back!" he started yelling as he reached towards his bag.

"Look, your sister is dead Louis. She's dead! And you need to take those tablets that were in your bag. Not taking them has clearly made you hallucinate!" James started yelling back in frustration.

Louis started walking towards us. Everyone else was stressed but I was terrified. No one knew what Louis was fully capable of, but me. He had me convinced that he cared about me, saved me, changed my mindset towards life, and then tried to kill me. I didn't want to meet him in the woods from the start.

I held James and whispered, "We've got to run. He's going to do something."

Don't forget,
We are not eternal...

"Louis, we're going to go now and you're going to let us. Okay? This was a waste of time," James said calmly.

"You ain't going nowhere! She's close to coming home. I'm gonna finish what I started. I have to. I want my sister back! My parents need my sister back," Louis got agitated.

The panic inside of me grew. I wanted to vanish. I didn't want to be there anymore. He tried killing me! And everyone needed to stop thinking they were dealing with a normal guy. Louis was manipulative and as theorised-maybe even... insane.

We were all standing there and Louis in front of us trying to get something out of his bag. We were so close to leaving. All I wanted to do was run and get away from Louis.

Seeing him after what happened the day before made me uncomfortable. I was scared of him. I was petrified of him. I felt betrayed by him.

Malcolm tried calming Louis down so we could leave without Louis trying to start a fight, "We're very sorry about your sister Louis. Believe me, I know how you feel okay. But trying to start another fight isn't going to work. There's four of us and one of you."

Louis was practically shaking with anger, "How the hell would you know how I feel? You raped her! You never

Don't forget,
We are not eternal...

loved her! How can you hurt someone you love like that? You drove her out of town, you prick!"

I felt James's hands tightening around mine after Louis questioned Malcolm's love for Ella. I realised James still felt responsible for my almost suicide but consoling him about it was the last thing on my mind.

I just wanted Louis to leave us alone.

Malcolm stayed pretty calm for what Louis had said to him and admitted to his faults, "Yeah Louis. I raped her. I know. I fucking know! Do you think I don't think about it every day? I do! I wish I could take it back. I wish I could redo things. I raped her, I hurt her because I loved her but she didn't love me. What can I say? My anger got the better of me.

But she killed herself, Louis. Okay? She jumped off the pier. And it's my fault. It's all my fault. I should have never done what I did to her. My love for her is what killed her. I loved in a fucked-up way. I let my love for her control my anger. And it's because of that, she jumped off the pier.

Nothing else. No one else. Me!" Malcolm had become teary and his voice was starting to tremble. It made me realise that he had to deal with so much more guilt than I ever did. His strength in staying alive after his

Don't forget,
We are not eternal...

involvement with Ella made me feel somewhat proud of him.

As horrible as it sounds, Malcolm survived his guilt even though it still haunted him. He wronged Ella by forcing her, but I knew he didn't deserve to die for it. Deep down I knew the incident had changed him into a better person.

"I'm the cause of so much pain. I know! I didn't just hurt her. I hurt you! You lost a sister. Your parents lost a daughter. People lost their friend. And now, there's a chain of how many people you're hurting because of your sister's death. And her death is probably what's making you think this," Malcolm slowly walked towards Louis. I think Malcolm was trying to comfort him – after all, Malcolm also understood the pain of losing Ella.

"I know you think your sister is alive and just out of town or something. But please just take a moment to understand how ludicrous that sounds. We were all told that she jumped off the pier. She left a letter. She's passed, Louis. She'll always be in our hearts but we shouldn't let the grief control our lives," Malcolm's words were also teaching me how to move on from the incident.

Louis had calmed down a little. But not enough. He replied to Malcolm, "You're wrong Mal. You all think

Don't forget,
We are not eternal...

she's dead. But she's alive and she will come back... if you guys aren't here."

Louis's delusions became worrying to everyone. Especially me.

Abruptly, Piper yelled out a line that changed our lives forever...

"Malcolm watch out, he's got a knife!"

Don't forget,
We are not eternal...

Chapter 24

A knife

Amelia Contritum

*Life can take unexpected turns
Make the most of it whilst you still can.*

"What! Why the fuck do you have a knife!" Malcolm yelled as he swiftly ran away from Louis back to where the rest of us were standing. Everyone cautiously started walking back away from the cleared area - further away from the car. And into the deep end of the woods...

My stomach tightened and my body froze in fear - he was going to kill us. He was going to kill us. I knew going to meet him was a dreadful idea from the start.

He started pacing faster towards us. We were like cattle awaiting our slaughter. We had nothing. No knife. No vase to hit his head. No time to reach for the phone and call the police. No way to run to the car. He was in front and we could only move to the end of the clearing and into the woods.

"We have to run!" I screamed when Louis ran towards us. My legs didn't work. I didn't know where to go. My whole body was shaking and fatigued because of all the adrenaline that had gathered up since the car ride.

"James grab him!" Malcolm yelled.

"What the fuck are they doing?" Piper shouted.

James and Malcolm both ran to Louis from the right and left to push him down. Piper and I stood in shock near the entering of the woods whilst the boys decided to charge towards a guy holding a knife.

Life can take unexpected turns
Make the most of it whilst you still can.

My anxiety increased. I felt sick. I wanted to cry. What the hell were we doing there?

"Amy!" James called out as he and Malcolm both tackled Louis like a rugby player and threw the knife towards me, "Throw the knife away!"

I grabbed the devil touched knife and threw it as far I could into the woods.

"Piper, run to my car and get it started quickly. We'll be there soon," James threw his keys to Piper and she started running back to the car.

"What do we do with him?" I asked as I walked towards them. Louis kept trying to escape from Malcolm's and James's tight grip.

"Hey, Amelia!" Louis stared me deep in the eyes, "Thought you should know one thing."

"Shut the fuck up, you bastard!" Malcolm took a swing whilst Louis was talking. I didn't want to see Louis hurt like that. All I wanted was to be back at home with James and far away from this mess.

"Let him finish," I said in respect to Louis's emotional pain.

"I kept my promise, Amelia... I kept one. You got to meet the poet of that nature poem before you died..."

Life can take unexpected turns
Make the most of it whilst you still can.

Before I died... I was confused. What was he talking about?

"Amy, move!" James let go of Louis leaving him in the hands of Malcolm and rushed to me.

I turned around.

What was all the commotion about? I thought.

And when I expected to see the empty woods that stood behind me, I saw Louis's sanity instead.

"No!" James screamed as my body fell onto the ground and my love ran to me - my body which had the devil touched knife pierced into my stomach.

One last pinprick of pain as the knife ruined all my chances of a happy life. Stabbed into my stomach, with all my blood pouring over me for the last time. My last encounter with any sort of knife. My too often spilled blood dripped over my body for the last time.

I felt James's hands around me, his breathing was shaky, just like his hands were shaking in disbelief.

"Stay with me Amelia!" his voice echoed, yelling for help and begging me to survive the one time I had no control. "Jaz, love. Please, you gotta fight for your life here! Stay strong one more time. Please don't leave me. I love you!"

Life can take unexpected turns
Make the most of it whilst you still can.

"I... I love you too... J... Jammy boy..." I stuttered as the stabbing pain disputed between my life and my death.

My head which laid on his lap, felt James's tears drip on to my cheek. His watery eyes. His beautiful, emerald-green eyes looked at mine for the last time.

And my eyes?

For the few blinks I could force myself to, my eyes, for the final time they could see, they saw my killer:

Ella...

Life can take unexpected turns
Make the most of it whilst you still can.

Chapter 25
A letter

Ella Reco

*Don't let love ruin you to the extent,
That you ruin it for someone else...*

Louis,

What I'm gonna tell you is very important and you can't tell anyone.

I'm skipping town. I don't think I can stay here anymore Louis. I can't stand this place. Something bad happened. There are too many messed up feelings attached to this town. Malcolm raped me yesterday and his friend James sat downstairs knowing what Malcolm was doing to me and did nothing.

By the time I escaped, Piper Jackson and Amelia Contritum were sat on the bench near the house. They saw me crying and running from Malcolm/Piper's house. They stopped me and asked what was wrong.

I was worried Malcolm was going to chase after me so I told them what he did to me. I was in shock, Amelia told me to go to the police but Piper intervened. To keep her twin brother from going to prison she threatened to leak videos of me. They would make my life a living hell if I stayed here. Louis, I can't. I'm sorry but I can't.

Please don't tell anyone this, especially since I'm still alive. And about that, you have to tell everyone that I took my own life. I'll write a fake suicide note to make everyone believe I'm dead. I'll make the letter out to be like I jumped off the pier, that way if my

Don't let love ruin you to the extent,
That you ruin it for someone else...

body isn't found, they won't question it too much because of the currents and tides.

I'm begging you; no one can find out I'm still alive. Not even mum and dad. I trust you but you have to trust me when I say that I'm not safe to come back home as long as Malcolm, Piper, Amelia, and James are still here.

I love you, Lou Lou, but I need to heal after what happened.

I can't stop thinking about what happened. The weight of his body pushing me down and my helplessness is haunting me. The way Malcolm used all his strength to keep me down whilst he stripped me bare and touched me even though I begged him not to.

I can't stay here.

I'm so sorry

- **Ella**

Ps- If you need to reach me in an absolute emergency, I'll leave my number. Only call me if something bad has happened or if I'm safe to come home.

07659124388

Don't let love ruin you to the extent,
That you ruin it for someone else...

Words from the writer

Honestly, I just have one thing to say.

Never ever give up!

Whether its life, it's a hobby or it's a dream. Just keep trying. If no one has said this to you, just know *I* have faith in you.

With lots of love,

Sanaa Dal x

Acknowledgements

- **Fowziyah Adam,** thank you for the illustrations of this book especially in such a small frame of time. I'm so grateful x

- **David Foster,** thank you for never getting tired of me when I'd run up the stairs to your office breathless and (knock on the door a little too hard my hand would hurt), and then ask you to spend most of your lunchtime giving me feedback on my writing even though you were busy. PS. I'm still waiting for your finished book...

- **Aiza Asif,** I'd never have been able to create my final drafts and perfect this book without your great editing skills. I'm truly grateful. Who else would agree to call me in the middle of the night to help me determine the characters and the plot of this story?

- **Humaira Bhuta,** for motivating me every time I'd feel like giving up. Without you listening every time I complained about something in this book. I'm sure I would have given up without you convincing me to finish it off to see where it could go.

- **Fatima Bhayat,** who persuaded me to think deeper into the plot of the story. Thank you for always helping me with this story in the middle of our health and social lessons.

Illustrations by Fowziyah Adam

To my first love,

    Utseende, ditt. Och färgerna lyser

    Glaset var fixat. Mitt hjärta strålade.

    Och mitt leende utstrålade,

    Vårt skratt ekade...

    Min älskade älskling

    Du lärde mig kärlek

    Du fångade mitt hjärta och nu...

    Mitt hjärta kommer alltid att vara ditt

    Hur ska jag kunna leva utan dig?

    Jag kommer alltid att älska dig min älskling

Från ditt solsken (nummer 24)

    Sanaa Dal

About the Author

'Sanaa Dal wrote her first book (Poisoned Love) at the age of 15, whilst still at high school. She was inspired by negative attitudes towards suicide and self-harm. The theme of her first book, which is fictional, follows the consequences wrongful anger can have. And more importantly, her work strongly focuses on coping mechanisms. Mechanisms that a large percentage of youths and young adults today resort to. Such as self-harm, substance abuse, and even dark humour to cope with any stress, guilt or trauma people go through.

You can reach her on her Instagram @sanaadal or email, sanaa.dal@outlook.com'

Lightning Source UK Ltd.
Milton Keynes UK
UKHW011013210820
368606UK00001B/75